STONE FALL

A Stone Cold Thriller

J. D. WESTON

ACKNOWLEDGMENTS

Authors are often portrayed as having very lonely work lives. There breeds a stereotypical image of reclusive authors talking only to their cat or dog and their editor, and living off cereal and brandy.

I beg to differ.

There is absolutely no way on the planet that this book could have been created to the standard it is without the help and support of Erica Bawden, Paul Weston, Danny Maguire, and Heather Draper. All of whom offered vital feedback during various drafts and supported me while I locked myself away and spoke to my imaginary dog, ate cereal and drank brandy.

The book was painstakingly edited by Ceri Savage, who continues to sit with me on Skype every week as we flesh out the series, and also threw in some amazing ideas.

To those named above, I am truly grateful.

J.D. Weston.

GET J.D.WESTON'S STARTER LIBRARY FOR FREE

Stay up to date with the Stone Cold Thriller series and get FREE eBooks sent straight to your inbox.

Details can be found at the end of this book.

1

FALLEN ANGEL

Two men sat in a black cab outside St Leonard's Primary School. The driver looked like any other black cab driver and took the same fare every day. He was dressed for comfort in trainers, a t-shirt and jogging bottoms, just like he did on most days. The other man sat in the large rear space with an open newspaper and flicked through the trashy photos of celebrities. He wore a pair of jeans and a loose jacket over an open-necked polo shirt.

All around them were mums and friends chatting while they waited to collect their children from school. The women stood in groups of two or three making idle small talk between glances at the front doors of the large brick building. They were waiting for the first opportunity to break away from the meaningless chat and get back home to their lives.

Among the mums were several men, not dads, but drivers, who stood unsmiling beside their cars. The school was private, well-regarded and extremely expensive.

The driver had parked a hundred yards back from the main gate, close enough for the little girl to see the cab, but far enough away from the eyes of prying mothers.

The main doors opened, and dozens of uniformed kids ran out towards the waiting arms of their mums. They showed pictures they had painted during class, some opened tupperware boxes to display the cakes they had baked and passed their mums their bags to carry for them. Other kids met their drivers and simply climbed into the back of the car without conversation.

"You'll never get away with this," said the driver to the man in the back. "She's just a kid."

"Relax, she is merely a pawn," said the man in the back seat. "Just like your family, Mr Bell. I have no use for them, but sometimes we need a little..." he paused, "*encouragement*. I have far greater ambitions, Mr Bell, than anything to do with the lives of young children. I deal in nations. So much grander, don't you think?"

"But she won't recognise you, you'll scare her," the driver replied.

"Inshallah, by the time she opens the door it will be too late."

The intuition of the man in the rear paid off. A short while later the door was opened by a little girl, and she climbed in.

"Hey, who are you?" she said.

""Oh, you must be Angel?" said the man in the back. "It's okay, I am helping, Mr Bell today. Why don't you close the door, it's cold outside, yes?"

Angel turned and pulled the heavy door closed, before settling herself onto the seat.

"Do you need help with the seatbelt?"

"No, I can do it myself, I do it every day."

"Oh, well you must be a very clever girl then, Angel. Drive on."

The driver indicated, pulled away from the kerb and joined the slow moving traffic.

"So," said the man in the back, "tell me about your day, Angel. Did you make a painting? Or cook a cake?"

"You don't make a painting, you paint a painting, and you don't cook a cake, you bake a cake."

The man laughed. "Such a clever girl, you know when I went to school, we didn't learn such things."

"Where did you go to school?"

"A long way from here, Angel. Somewhere very far away, but it is always in my heart, and I can find my way home with my eyes closed. Is this place in your heart, Angel?"

"My school?"

"Yes, your school, your friends and the city. Do you love them?"

"I love my friends, but not my school."

"And the city, Angel? Do you love London?"

"I don't know, I haven't been anywhere else, so I don't know what's better."

"You really are a very clever girl for somebody so young."

"How do you know how old I am?" Angel asked.

"Oh, Angel, we know all about you. And your Mum."

"Where are we going? This isn't the way."

"I must be honest with you, Angel, we are going for a little holiday. Perhaps afterwards you will know if you miss your home or not."

The man was busy pouring a liquid from a small plastic bottle onto a handkerchief.

"Where are we going? What's that you're doing?" asked Angel. "I want my mum."

"Little girl, you have asked too many questions. It's nap time."

2

THE EYES OF THE BEAST

ORDINARY PEOPLE WALKED PAST WHERE HARVEY SAT, THEY led ordinary lives, had ordinary jobs, wore ordinary clothes and had ordinary reasons for being there.

Harvey was far from ordinary. He wore casual clothes, tan boots, black cargo pants and a plain white t-shirt underneath his leather bikers jacket, and he sat in a coffee shop amongst ordinary people on Queen Victoria Street in the city of London. But he was looking for the extraordinary.

He'd been sat for over an hour, observing.

His ear-piece was barely visible unless somebody was looking for it. It crackled into life.

"Stone, how are you doing there?" It was Melody Mills, his colleague.

He scratched his face and discreetly tapped the button twice to confirm nothing had happened yet.

"We're doing another pass along Cannon Street, keep your eyes open and shout if you see him."

He was looking for an ordinary man in an ordinary world with an extraordinary reason for being in London.

A group of four women walked past the coffee shop,

where Harvey sat by the window in the corner with his back to the wall. Protecting his back was an old habit, part of his past life, back when he'd looked over his shoulder more than he looked in front.

The women laughed and joked at something one of them was showing on her phone, and they walked on carefree.

Two men in suits passed them walking in the opposite direction. One of the men, a short, stocky man in a tight suit and long heavy jacket casually turned to admire them walking away then continued on. The man turned to keep up with his friend and bumped shoulders with another man in jeans, trainers and an oversized fleece jacket. His hair was shaved bald, and a tattoo crawled up his neck. He carried a rucksack slung over both shoulders and walked with his hands in his jacket pockets at a faster than average speed.

Harvey stood up, left the coffee shop and began to follow the bald man along Queen Victoria Street. The man crossed over Bread Street, where he passed the group of girls without looking or admiring, then crossed to the other side of Queen Victoria Street. Harvey stayed on his side of the road, but matched the man's pace, giving the impression he was heading somewhere ordinary like the hundreds of other people in view. It was London, and hiding in plain sight was fairly simple if you acted ordinarily.

The man turned into Lambeth Hill, a quieter road that led down to Upper Thames Street. Harvey crossed the road after him, dodging between taxis and cars as the man disappeared from sight. He sprinted across the last few lanes of traffic and up to the corner of Lambeth Hill then resumed his brisk walk. He turned the corner but saw nothing ahead. Harvey discreetly checked around him, in doorways and alleyways, nothing. The street was empty of cars and people. Harvey began to run.

"Stone, you're on the move, we saw your tracker, you have eyes on him?" said Mills.

Harvey began to jog. "Lambeth Hill, heading down to Upper Thames Street, he's on foot moving fast, jeans and a blue fleece, shaved head and carrying a rucksack."

"Reg has you on-screen, we're on Puddle Dock coming onto Upper Thames Street now."

"Target has disappeared," said Harvey.

"You lost him?"

Harvey didn't reply.

Harvey picked up the pace of his run. He rounded a corner and caught a glimpse of the man ahead turning onto Upper Thames Street, heading toward Mills and the team. He was running.

"I've got eyes on him, he's onto me, he's running toward you on Upper Thames-"

"Okay, we have a visual."

Harvey heard the roar of the team's Audi a hundred yards away, followed by the screech of tyres on tarmac. He sprinted to the end of the road to see the man running across the four-lane street, then disappear into a cobbled road between two buildings that led to the waterside. Angry drivers honked their horns, and other cars skidded to avoid crashing into the mass of stopped traffic. Harvey leapt across a car bonnet and narrowly missed being hit by another vehicle skidding to a halt in the next lane.

Melody was a hundred yards ahead, running away from the man into an alleyway to cut him off.

Harvey reached the riverside, he looked left then right, and saw the tattooed man running across the Millennium Bridge above him. Melody was fifty yards behind him sprinting hard between groups of tourists. Harvey carried on running and made his way onto the bridge but by the time he reached it, he was well behind Melody and the man.

By the time Harvey reached the centre of the bridge, crowds of people blocked his path. He called out to them, "Move, move, move," and barged through the barrier of pedestrians. He reached the middle of a crowd where people were stopped and staring, men and women held their phones up making a video of the scene. Harvey broke through to find the man standing with a machete to Melody's throat.

"Let her go, Victor," said Harvey. "What's she done to you?"

"What's she done to me?" Victor replied. "You think I don't know you guys have been watching me?" Victor was shaking, he was at breaking point.

Harvey didn't reply.

"It ends now, right here."

"*You* don't tell *me* when it ends, Victor."

Victor looked surprised.

"You think I'm going to play into your hands?" began Harvey. "You think I'm going to tell you what you want to hear, Victor? You think this is a movie? Well it's not, you're holding a machete to my friend's throat, and you have two possible outcomes." Harvey stopped and stared at him, then spoke calmly at the man. "You drop the machete, she arrests you, you live–"

"And if I don't, you're gonna take this off me and kill me in front of all these people?"

"I haven't decided if you die yet, Victor," replied Harvey, "that's your gamble isn't it?" Harvey gave an almost imperceptible nod to Melody, who smashed her head back into Victor's nose. The man released his hold just enough for her to move away from him, and twist his left arm back in one smooth action. But Victor was stronger than he looked. He pulled Melody's arm away, released her grip on him and grabbed her hair. He wrenched her head back, and with his right hand swung the machete back, ready to land the blade on her neck.

Harvey pounced forwards and tackled Victor while his arm was swung back. He pinned him against the railing and crunched his forehead down onto the man's nose. Victor swung again, this time at Harvey, but Harvey stepped into the swing, blocked Victor's arm and ripped the weapon from the bald man's hands. Harvey turned the blade and, with a flick of his wrist, jammed it down into Victor's arm. The sharp, heavy knife sliced through the man's wrist like it was cutting bananas from a tree. The hand fell uselessly to the floor.

Victor doubled over in agony, and Melody reached out to cuff his good hand, but he saw it coming and stood upright, sucking in air between his gritted teeth.

"Are you coming easy, Victor?" said Melody. "Don't make this any harder than it needs to be."

Harvey pulled his Sig. "On the ground, now," he shouted at Victor.

"I have to," said Victor. "They have my son," he reached for the bloodied cuff of his ruined arm.

"Don't move, Victor, put your arm down now," shouted Harvey. "Melody get those people out of here," he continued, not releasing his eyes from Victor's.

"Who has him, Victor? We can help," said Harvey.

Melody turned, and shouted to the crowds, "Move back, get out of here, come on, move back."

"They'll kill him if I don't-"

"Victor, talk to me."

The noise of the crowd control fell to a distant hum in the background of Harvey's concentration, only the dull thud of his heartbeat in his ears played in his mind. Victor stopped with the fingers of his left hand hidden inside the right-hand cuff. Harvey glanced down and saw the small switch and two thin wires.

Tears began to roll down Victor's face. He looked up at the sky, and his fingers stumbled in the sticky mess.

Harvey fired.

His two shots found Victor's forehead. It had been a risk. Victor could have still hit the switch, but if Harvey hadn't fired, he would have *definitely* hit the switch.

Victor fell to his knees, his hand still on the little bundle of wires that stuck out of his cuff. Before his body had a chance to fall to the ground and possibly blow them all sky high, Harvey stepped forwards and caught him, then with a grunt, he hoisted the man over the handrail.

The dead body plummeted to the river below and landed face down. There was no explosion. There was no surge of water. There was no more Victor Hague.

3

GREEN EYED MONSTER

FAISAL BIN YASSER AL SAYAN LEANED AGAINST A STOLEN
black taxi in a mechanic's garage in Stratford, East London.
There were three taxis in total, all parked side by side in the
narrow space. The warehouse was an open space, cluttered
with car parts, such as gearboxes, exhausts and engine blocks,
arranged in no particular fashion. To the right-hand side of
the space were four rooms built from concrete blocks with
heavy wooden doors. Each room was twelve-foot square.
Door number one stood ajar, door two was locked and doors
three and four were also open.

Stood beside Al Sayan was Angel. She looked up at him
and then around at the dirty garage.

Al Sayan took a phone from his pocket and dialled a
number from memory. The ringtone was answered quickly,
but no voice offered a greeting.

"I know you're there," said Al Sayan, "I can hear you
breathing."

"Where is she?"

"All in good time," said Al Sayan.

"Who are you?"

"Oh you'll know me when we meet, but until then-"

"You're messing with the wrong person."

"Is that correct?" asked Al Sayan. "I believe it is me who will call the shots, as you say. Let's keep the childish threats out of this, it is purely business, something I understand you are extremely good at."

"What do you want? Money?"

"Do not insult me, I am no petty criminal."

"Tell me what you want, it's yours, but harm her, and I'll make sure you suffer."

"How very boring," said Al Sayan. "We have a mutual friend. Or should I say, we had a mutual friend? Until this morning."

"Hague?"

"Ah, so you watch the news, it was exciting wasn't it? He was supposed to complete a task, after which I would release his child," said Al Sayan. "He failed his task, as you know."

"And his child?"

Al Sayan tutted. "Such a waste of life."

"Tell me what you want, I haven't failed yet."

"I know, Victor spoke very highly of you, I believe we shared a shipment."

"He's got a big mouth."

"He had a big mouth," corrected Al Sayan. "He also told me you are planning something. I'm not a collector, but I am very interested in ancient artefacts."

"So go to the museum."

"No, not my style. Something as valuable as the item you have your eye on could fund my little project."

"Your little project?"

"Let's just say, I'm cleaning this city, this country. It is filthy."

"So leave, go back to wherever it is you came from."

"It is not that simple I'm afraid. I just couldn't sleep at night knowing of all the sinners walking freely here." Al Sayan paused. "You could help me. We'd make a great team."

"I won't help you,"

"Then I am afraid little Angel here will die a very painful death." He looked down at the little girl who cried out. "You hear her?" said Al Sayan.

"I do, let me talk to her."

"No, you need to earn that."

"You're a sick son of a bitch."

"Wrong again, what I am is dedicated."

"So I do the job for you, and you give me my daughter back?"

"That's the gist of it, but there is one more thing," said Al Sayan. "An obstacle."

"What is it?"

"How closely did you watch the news of our mutual friend?"

"I have an eye for detail."

"So you would have seen the hero?"

"He's known to me."

"I know he is. He's your obstacle, I want him out of the picture," said Al Sayan, "and his friends, they're already too close."

"How do you expect me to do that?"

"I have already made plans for Mr Stone, he has ruined my plans once too often. He will be running now, so you should find it easy. The buddha arrives today and will be locked in the vault. The auction is in four days. In exactly two days time I will be creating quite a large diversion, somewhere close to the auction. The chaos will provide a means of escape for you and your team. Your death or capture will result in our little Angel here growing wings earlier than expected."

"Don't you-"

Al Sayan disconnected the call.

4

THE PACK

FRANK CARVER STOOD OUTSIDE HIS OFFICE ON THE mezzanine floor in the team's headquarters. He looked down and watched as his team arrived. Headquarters was a brick building beside the Thames Barrier in Silvertown, East London. It stood alone in a compound surrounded by a high wall and electric gates. The team occupied half the building, the other half belonged to the team of engineers that ran the barrier on a daily basis.

Frank's team was a specialist black ops team that reported to the Home Office, via MI5. They were not the balaclava-clad assault team that would abseil down buildings and storm into hostage situations or terrorist cells. They were a very small team of highly skilled individuals. Each of them was a specialist in their own field, and collectively they worked domestic organised crime investigations, while SO10 and other units dealt with the rising terrorist threats. The thinking behind Frank's unit was that while the well known and well-funded black ops operatives stormed buildings and kicked the doors in of terrorist cells, the organised crime world was left wide open for gangs and criminals to run amok. The growth in organised crime since 9/11 and 7/7 was big enough to warrant charging a few highly-skilled operatives with the task of keeping the organised crime world at bay. The team let these criminals know that they didn't have free reign. Taking down the ring-leaders and, most importantly, shutting the doors of sources to prevent crimes happening again was their main objective.

Denver Cox drove the brand new VW Transporter into the HQ building. He parked between Harvey's BMW motor-cycle and the team's Audi in the engineering area immediately to the left of the large sliding shutter doors. The engineering area was his own domain. He was the driver, the mechanic and the engineer, plus he was an expert pilot in both fixed-wing aircraft and helicopter.

Denver stepped out of the brand new van and stretched. He'd been in the seat for the entire day. The van was black with tinted windows, and had been significantly fixed up by Denver. He'd dropped the diesel engine out and replaced it with a four-litre V6. He'd upgraded the suspension, put bigger wheels on and improved the brakes. From the outside, it looked like a standard VW Transporter, but with Denver at the wheel, it could keep up with most cars on the road. It was an ideal team vehicle.

Each team member had a specific skill set, and the Home Office had furnished them all with the tools required for the job. Denver had his engineering area, Melody had her armoury, and Reg had his command centre, which consisted of twelve wall-mounted twenty-four inch screens and his own computer software and hardware creation.

Melody Mills was a surveillance expert and sniper, plus she was as smart as they come. She had aced every exam she had ever taken and worked her way up from entry level constabulary. After spending a few years as a detective, she was then pulled into SO10 where she met Frank. She was thirty years old and led the team's operations.

Denver opened the rear door for Reg to step out. Reg Tenant was just closing down his two computers that lived permanently inside the van. He climbed out and walked over to his command centre which was immediately to the right of the sliding shutter doors.

Frank led the team. He was a highly experienced investigator who had worked his way through the constabulary and several detective units, eventually leading an organised crime division of SO10 before being given the chance to run a team of specialists. He was in his fifties, and if he wasn't thinking about the case they were working on, he was thinking about his retirement.

The covert team performed almost the same function as his SO10 team had, but without the restrictions of a government organisation. He was answerable to the Home Office and MI5, but aside from that, nobody knew of them. The team's existence wasn't public knowledge. It couldn't be, if the public were aware of them, there would be uproar. They weren't licensed to kill, per se, but they were licensed to get the job done.

Frank was happy with his team. It was still early days, and they needed a little guidance, but they worked well together and got the job done, and that was important for both the team's success and Frank's retirement.

Frank hadn't always been an honest cop. In fact, he barely remembered the days when he'd been green and keen. He'd been tangled up in the criminal world's web of deceit for far too long. Often, a favour from one criminal led to him risking his job in return, which required another favour from another criminal. The cycle had been endless. Until, twelve months previously, when he'd watched through a window in the blackest of nights, as Harvey Stone had killed the man who held Frank's balls in his hands. The man had been Terry Thomson, the renowned East End villain.

Shortly afterwards, Frank had discovered the body of a man that Harvey had boiled to death, laying in an old copper bath in the basement of Harvey's foster father's house. It had been the man Harvey had searched for more than twenty years; his sister's other rapist. Sitting beside the corpse on the cold stone floor was the missing sex offender that Harvey had left to Frank as a gift. He had been tied to a wooden beam in the cellar alongside the still-steaming, old copper bath.

On the grounds of the estate, Frank had also found a transit van full of Heckler and Koch MP5s that he'd been looking for, another gift from Harvey.

A bad man would have killed the sex offender, sold the guns on the black market and continued his life of crime. But Harvey had left all those gifts for Frank then retired to a little farm in the south of France. He'd escaped the life of crime, that was how Frank knew that Harvey wanted out. It was how he knew that the good inside him was stronger than the evil. It had been at a time when Frank was forming the team. They had the brains, a sniper and surveillance. They had the driver, pilot and mechanic. They had the tech guru. But they had needed someone with the skills that can't be taught. Someone who didn't mind getting their hands dirty, for the right reasons. That someone had been Harvey.

So given the choice of prison or working for the team, Harvey had opted to work for the team. It had been a difficult transition. Harvey had spent his entire life surrounded by criminals and avoiding the law, and now he was adjusting. Harvey was guided by his moral compass, which was true and straight but lacked experience of the formalities. Frank was helping him adjust.

Frank had promised to help Harvey find out the reasons behind his best friend Julios' murder and his parent's deaths, their names and where they were buried, so that Harvey could move on with his life. Until then, Harvey was on a leash, and prison loomed over him like an angry black cloud.

Frank watched Harvey step from the van and walk casually over to his desk. He was a fearsome man, Frank thought. Harvey wasn't an oversized muscle head, he was athletic but strong. His confidence carried across the room wherever he walked, and people stopped and stared like the devil had passed them by.

Harvey didn't have large, wall-mounted monitors. He didn't have a tool chest or cabinets with automatic weapons and surveillance equipment. Harvey had a small desk for his laptop and a chair. Behind it was his punch bag, which hung from the mezzanine floor above. Harvey's needs were basic.

"Stone, Mills, my office," Frank called down to them.

5

UNLEASH THE BEAST

"Debrief?" said Frank, looking at Harvey.

Harvey didn't reply.

"So we lost Victor Hague," said Frank. It wasn't a question. He had overheard the comms between the team, and then he'd seen the resulting media reports. 'Breaking news. Unknown security organisation tackles terrorist with an explosive vest on London's Millennium Footbridge.' The video had been captured by a nearby tourist.

"He was loaded, sir," said Melody, "his backpack-"

"I can imagine what he was wearing, Mills," interrupted Frank, "but now we've lost our way in to the explosives supplier, and will need to start again."

"He would have been gone anyway, sir. He was going to blow something up, people, it's the city, sir. It would have been a disaster."

"Agreed, so what do we have to go on?"

Harvey tossed a plastic shopping bag onto Frank's desk.

"What's that, Stone?" asked Frank, keeping his tone calm, but secretly outraged by having somebody throw a bag onto his desk rather than pass it to him in a more civilised fashion.

"Hague's hand," replied Harvey.

"His what?"

"His hand."

"You cut it off?"

"It was either that, or he would have cut Melody's head off, in front of hundreds of members of the public," said Harvey.

"He put a machete to my throat, sir," said Melody, by way of confirmation.

"Yes, I saw the footage, someone recorded it and sent it to the BBC. Nice of them, eh? They didn't show the hand, oddly enough."

Harvey and Melody were silent.

"What's the plan with it?"

"With what, sir?"

"The hand, Melody, are we going to stuff it and stick it on the wall?"

"No, sir, but we thought it prudent to take it away from the general public."

"Can Reg do anything with it?"

"Just prints, sir, but we already know what Hague was involved in, I can't see it telling us anything else."

"Okay, print it, and send it off to wherever they have the rest of him. Then get everyone in the meeting room."

A short while later the team walked up the stairs to the meeting room and assumed their positions. Reg sat on one of the sofas, Denver sat on the arm of the other sofa, Melody stood near the coffee machine, and Harvey leaned on the wall by the door. Frank stood at the head of the room by the two whiteboards.

"Firstly, team, thank you all for your efforts this morning, we managed to avert a potential disaster, and there is one less bad guy on the loose. However...." Frank inhaled deeply. "There are two pieces of slightly not so good news."

The team were all listening intently.

"We cannot take credit for today's actions. We are, as you know, informal, we don't exist. SO10 will take the credit. Secondly, and far more importantly, we no longer have an in into Hague's world, and ladies and gentlemen, without Hague we won't know when the next shipment will be coming. But we can be quite certain that the first shipment has already been distributed."

"How does that concern us?" asked Melody, "Surely that's a job for Customs and Excise."

"Typically, yes, however one of the buyers is known to us and falls under our jurisdiction," replied Frank.

The team thought on who might want explosives.

"Want a clue?" asked Frank.

The team were quiet.

"My theory is that the explosives sold to our man will be used to blow a vault door."

"Not people then?" asked Melody.

"No, Mills, not people, that would be terrorism, and as you pointed out earlier, that does not fall under our jurisdiction." Frank put the whiteboard marker down and walked to the front of the table, where he sat back and leaned on the edge. "Hague had his fingers in many pies, all different flavours. Our particular pie is quite straightforward. I had Reg analyse Hague's phone records. Lots of data, most of it useless. Untraceable phones, unknown owners, short calls, coded messages. Mostly garbage." Frank cleared his throat. "However, one number that Hague had been talking to had contacted somebody we all known, who has evaded us for many years. Somebody who targets diamonds and art, and somebody who, with the right amount of plastic explosives, could get into any vault."

"Who, sir?" asked Reg. "The suspense is killing me."

"Not yet, Tenant," replied Frank. "First I want to paint a

picture." Frank hit the space bar on his laptop, which was connected by HDMI to the TV in the room. A photo of a small, green Chinese buddha appeared on the large screen.

"Can anyone tell me what this is?" asked Frank.

"A scented candle?" said Reg.

Melody smiled. "It's a buddha, sir. By the colouring, I'd say it was jade, and by the condition, I'd say it was old."

"Good," said Frank. "It *is*, in fact, an ancient jade buddha. How old?" He offered the question to the room.

"Five hundred years," said Denver.

"Older."

"Seven hundred and fifty," asked Reg.

"Older."

"Fifteen hundred?" asked Melody, her eyebrows raised in doubt.

Frank looked at her, then paused. "Older," he said quietly.

"Two thousand years?" asked Denver.

"Give or a take a century, experts can't date it accurately."

"This is fun," said Reg. "What's the next question?"

"Why am I showing you it?" asked Frank.

"It's a target," said Melody. "You think somebody's going to steal it?"

"Two points to Mills," replied Frank. "The two-thou-sand-year-old jade buddha is going up for auction later this week."

"Where?" asked Denver.

"Cornish House, out in deepest darkest Essex according to a website I found this morning."

"Essex?" said Denver, "Why there?"

"You'll see when you go. It's an old English manor house, surrounded by miles and miles of greenery with no tunnels, a large vault and no possible way of escaping. The owner is of English gentry and is a keen collector of art."

"So how do we know it's going to be stolen?" asked Reg.

"You'll see," said Frank. "How much do we think it's worth?" Frank offered the question to the room again.

"Ten million?" asked Denver.

"Twenty million," said Reg.

"You're both wrong," said Frank. "The item has never actually been bought or sold. It's been passed down through generations in a particular family of the aristocracy, and the starting bid price has not yet been disclosed."

"So how does anyone know how much money to bring to the auction?" asked Reg.

"For somebody so intelligent, you do ask some stupid questions, Tenant," said Frank. "Buyers of this type of artefact do not turn up to an auction with any money at all. In fact, the only people invited to the auction are ten of Europe's biggest collectors, all with a combined net worth greater than many small countries."

"So there's no price?" asked Melody.

"Not yet, but it's known that all of the buyers want the piece, just how far they'll go is yet to be seen."

"Crazy," said Denver.

"So that's what, where and why," said Harvey, speaking up for the first time.

Frank turned to face Harvey. "Who do you think would want this more anything in the world?"

"Only one person I know who *could* pull the job off."

"Go on," said Frank, smiling at the suspense.

"Stimson," said Harvey.

"Adam Stimson. Bonus points to Stone," said Frank, smiling. "Hague's phone records showed contact with one number that is in direct communication with Adam Stimson on a daily basis. What does that tell us?"

"Stimson's active. He's smart," said Harvey, "He won't contact anyone himself, he has men that do things like that for him."

"So if Stimson needed a little bang for his next job-"

"He'd have his closest man arrange it, he wouldn't trust anyone else," said Harvey.

"So if we add two and two?" asked Frank.

"Stimson needs explosives for a vault, and coincidently a priceless buddha is up for auction," said Melody.

"Your job is to recce the manor house. There's a restaurant attached so maybe you can go for breakfast?" began Frank. "I want to know exactly how you'd get in and out. Once we have our own grounding, we should be able to put plans into action to stop Stimson. Maybe this time we'll actually catch him."

"What about the source of the explosives?" asked Denver.

"Good question, it's a great question in fact, but alas, it's not our problem."

"Customs and Excise?" asked Melody.

"Yes, but we need them on our side, they're already on our case about the human trafficking ring. If we find *any* information on the source of the explosives, we pass that on to them, I don't want internal enemies." Frank stood, put his hands in his pockets and waited for the team's attention. "Tenant, you'll be here in headquarters, I want information on Stimson's man. Stone, Mills, and Cox, you'll be visiting the manor house tomorrow morning. Like I said, I want to know exactly how *you* would do the job." He addressed the last part of the statement to Harvey.

"Lastly," said Frank as he opened the door and turned back to the room, "the auction is in four days. We have no information on when the buddha will arrive, so assume that the robbery will take place any time between now and then. Any questions?"

The room was silent.

"Good. Go get me Adam Stimson."

———

"Okay, Reg, all on eyes on you right now, I'm afraid, get us something to start on," said Melody.

There were standing at Reg's command centre.

"Righto, Melody, so let's recap, we're putting eyes and ears on Stimson's man. And I guess you all want a visual of the manor house?"

"Stimson will be in the last phases of his plan, we're well behind already," said Harvey.

"How can you be sure?" asked Melody.

"Well, Stimson is a known criminal, not just by the police, but in the world of the criminals too. He's extremely good at what he does, he's a planner. You know how I feel about planning–"

"Failure to plan is planning to fail," the team chorused.

"Exactly," said Harvey, ignoring his colleagues' efforts at making fun of him. "So you need to be aware of a few things here. Adam Stimson has never been arrested, he's never been to prison, and likely never will."

"Because he's too good?" asked Reg.

"Yeah, and he's careful, Reg," said Harvey. "He wouldn't even buy moody fags from a bloke in a pub let alone make calls to an explosives dealer. But there's one thing that I do know for certain."

"Go on," said Melody.

"He's a glory hunter," said Harvey. "He'll want the job done so precisely that he'll be on it himself. He doesn't just send men out to do jobs for him, he's involved. It's his plan, it's his way, or not at all. He's one of the smartest strategists you'll come across and will have back up plans for his back up plans. We don't just need one way of doing the job, we need to think of every way we'd do the job, and we don't have much time. Stimson's had the luxury of time."

"What makes you so sure?" asked Reg.

"A year ago, the Cartwrights and the Thomsons were both planning to do a diamond heist, you all know the one?"

"Right, yeah. The Stimson's got away with it in the end, didn't they?"

"Yep, the diamonds are still missing. You know why the Cartwrights and the Thomsons didn't actually succeed?"

The team looked at each other.

"Didn't you kill Terry Thomson?" asked Denver.

Harvey didn't reply to the question. Instead, he continued. "Because Adam Stimson is smart. He knew that the Cartwrights and the Thomsons would go after the diamonds, so he arranged for twenty-four Heckler and Koch MP5s to be lost, and end up in Thomson's possession. The Cartwrights bought twelve of them, leaving the other twelve with Thomson. This led both of them to believe they had the hardware to do the job, but each of them was so engrossed in stopping the other from doing the job, a gang war started. Meanwhile, guess who digs a neat little hole somewhere nobody thought of digging and walks off with the diamonds?"

"Adam Stimson?"

"Not a single shot fired," said Harvey. "He's a smart man."

"So do we have Stimson's phone?" asked Melody.

"Yep, we do as it happens," said Reg. "I've been monitoring it for ages, but nothing ever happens."

"Of course nothing happens. As long as Stimson knows we're listening, that phone will be clean," said Harvey.

"It's encrypted actually, I can see and access everything, but can't hear the calls. Military grade hardware, way out of our league without significant investment."

"Did you ever meet Stimson?" asked Melody. "You know, in your-"

"In my days as a criminal, Melody?" finished Harvey.

"*Nobody* ever met Adam Stimson, even John Cartwright never knew what he looked like. I told you, he's smart."

"But we have his phone, he can't be that smart."

"You have his phone because he lets you have his phone, that's why you won't find anything incriminating on there. Yeah, we'll get contacts, and we can isolate the links from his trusted inner circle to external contacts in the outer circle. But we'll never nail Stimson like that, and he knows we won't bother arresting his inner circle when it's him we really want."

"Smart," said Melody. "So who is his inner circle?"

"Who's the guy that made contact with Hague?" asked Harvey.

"Lucas Larson," said Reg. "Lifetime criminal. His last stretch was five years in Belmarsh for intimidating a witness and perverting the course of justice."

"Is that the only name we have to go on?" asked Harvey.

"So far," replied Reg. "I've got LUCY analysing his records to show his most frequent numbers to see what we've got. But I'm going to need some more time here to build a full picture," said Reg.

Harvey and Melody took the hint and walked away, each going to their own desks in opposite corners of the room.

Melody sat and unloaded her Sig Sauer. She placed the unused rounds back in the little cardboard box inside her ammo cabinet, then stripped the Sig. She turned on the lamp and pulled her cleaning kit from her desk drawer. Each weapon Melody fired was meticulously cleaned before being returned to the armoury.

Harvey put his own Sig on his desk, cracked his neck left then right, and stretched his arms up and around. His body felt tight after sitting in the coffee shop all morning. He turned and landed a left jab into the punch bag, followed with a right hook that sent the bag swinging up to a nearly horizontal position. It swung back towards him and Harvey stopped its return dead with an uppercut. Jumping up, he took a wide grip on the steel joist that supported the mezzanine floor above him. He did a few pull-ups without counting then dropped to the floor.

"How's that research coming on?" asked Frank from upstairs. "Doesn't sound like much is happening."

"I think I've found something," said Reg.

Harvey looked at his watch, it had been less than two minutes. He strolled over to Reg and stood beside him, Melody and Denver came to see what he'd found.

"The most common dialled numbers from Stimson's phone are here." Reg outlined a group of numbers pasted into a text file on the far left, lower screen. There were three numbers.

"Family?" asked Melody.

"I don't suppose Adam Stimson is much of a family man myself, but, he does appear to enjoy talking to his mum. This is her number here, not a burner, it's even registered to her name." Reg highlighted the number. "He calls her at least twice a day. The evening calls seem to be the longest, morning calls are probably trivial mother and son stuff. Would you agree we can eliminate this number?"

"I'd agree with that," said Melody. "Harvey?"

"I'm not sure what's meant by trivial mother and son stuff, but I'll take your word for it," said Harvey.

Melody sensed the awkward reply. It was an area that the team usually avoided as they knew Harvey had been searching for his real parents' killer for many years.

"I call my mum at least twice a day unless we're on a job someplace," said Denver. "I can hear it in her voice that it makes her day, so I just can't bear not to anymore."

"How often do you see her?" asked Harvey.

"Three or four times a week. She does a curry for us all on

the weekends and usually has a little something for me to take home if I swing by during the week."

"A curry at the weekend? Don't you have a roast dinner, Denver?" asked Reg.

"A roast? No, my mum's vegetarian, we get a killer curry, rice and homemade naan bread."

"In all this time I don't think I've ever heard you talk about your family," said Melody.

"You never asked before," said Denver.

"How about you, Reg? How often do you see your mum?" asked Melody.

"Oh, pfff, maybe once or twice."

"A week?" asked Denver.

"No, not that often."

"A month? You only see your mum once or twice a month?"

"No, a year, give or take."

"A year?" cried Melody.

"Yeah, what's wrong with that?"

"How often do you call her?"

"Once a month, maybe."

"Reg, the woman brought you into the world, take some time out and go see her."

"Most blokes are the same, except Denver," argued Reg.

"You only get one mum, Reg, look after her," said Denver.

"Maybe if she cooked for me, I'd go round more often."

"Maybe if you went round there-"

"Are we actually going to look at these names?" said Harvey.

"Sorry, Harvey, bit insensitive of us," said Denver.

"Not insensitive, but if we're going to talk about family lives and what we're doing for Christmas, I'll go home early. I've got better things to be doing than stand here listening to a load of old women talking."

"What exactly do you do at home, Harvey?" asked Reg. "I imagine you go home, sit down and stare at a blank wall, but I bet in reality you have a really crazy hobby that you keep secret, like knitting or something."

"I think about you a lot, Reg," said Harvey.

"*Me? Really?*"

"Yeah, with no skin on. Now show me what you found."

Both Melody and Denver smirked. Harvey was really beginning to take his place in the team. He filled a hole that needed filling but brought much more to the table than just muscle and bravado. Melody looked at him with one hand on the back of Reg's chair. She thought about how different he was than the guy Frank had described when he first put the idea of bringing an ex-hitman, who was born and bred to live on the wrong side of the law, into the team.

"So all these numbers here," said Reg, "are out. But these two here are still in the game." Reg was in his element, he loved pulling information out of nowhere and presenting his skills to the team. "This number especially gets dialled an average of fourteen times per day, that's Larson's."

"Fourteen times per day, who calls anyone fourteen times per day?" asked Denver.

"A rich man who has a number two. He's someone Stimson delegates to. A trustee," said Melody.

"Who does the other number belong to? And what else do we have on Larson?" asked Harvey.

"Well, Lucas Larson. No previous, forty-five years old, born and raised in Munich, then moved to Britain when he was eighteen," said Reg.

"So Stimson calls three people frequently, his mum, Larson, and who else?" asked Denver. "Would he even need anyone else?"

"Yes," Harvey cut in. "Stimson has Larson, who's probably highly intelligent, and capable of running the show himself, but is held to Stimson for some other reason. This other number is someone very unintelligent, but is likely pretty handy and never too far away from Stimson."

"His bodyguard?" asked Melody.

"I'd say so. If we're going to get to Stimson, we'll need to take this guy out. But if we're going to catch Stimson, we'll need to be all over Larson," said Harvey. "I'm telling you, if we get Larson, we'll stand a much better chance of getting as a shot at Stimson. Where does Hague fit into this?"

"He doesn't anymore, he was just the explosives supplier," said Reg. "Larson's contact."

"Okay, but remember what Hague said? He was going to blow himself up, and he told us he *had* to do it, they had his boy," said Harvey. "Is this two different crimes or what? Who had his boy? He *was* carrying a bag full of explosives, are we forgetting that?"

"We're talking about going after a diamond thief who is buying illegally imported explosives to perform domestic organised crime," said Frank, who was leaning over the railing above them and listening, "which is exactly why this team exists. Nothing else concerns us."

The team looked up at Frank.

"So what do we have?" asked Frank.

"We have a location, a motive, and a link to Stimson, via Larson," said Melody.

"I also have Larson's phone monitored."

"Who's the third guy?" asked Frank. "The third number on Stimson's phone."

"An unknown. Harvey thinks it's a bodyguard."

"Makes sense," said Frank. "Now what?"

"I'd say we take a visit to the manor house tomorrow morning, go for breakfast, scope the place and work out how they're going to do the job," said Melody. "Until we get out there, this is all speculation."

"We're tracking all three phones, so we'll know if they're on the move."

"The auction is in four days," said Frank. "Harvey, if you were going to rob the place, when would you do the robbery?"

"As soon as possible," replied Harvey.

6

SHEEP

"I NEED SOME AIR," SAID HARVEY. HE STRODE TOWARDS the single door beside Reg's command centre and stepped out into the cold November day. The wind off the river a hundred yards away bit into his skin as he walked down to the riverside to lean on the railing and watch the water.

"Penny for them?" said Melody, who came and stood beside him.

He turned to her. "We're missing something."

"It's always like this at the start of an investigation, we're still gathering intel."

"We're making up theories. We should be out there, gathering facts."

"Yeah, well, a little extra time on the intel makes gathering the facts a lot quicker. It's okay." She held a cup of coffee, and offered him some. "Coffee?"

"No thanks, I'm going to go for a run soon. Something's missing, I need to clear my head."

"You know," began Melody. "I never said it before, but I owe you thanks. Actually, I owe you a few thanks, you saved my life." Six months ago, Melody had been captured during a human trafficking investigation. She'd been stripped of her clothes, had her hands tied and been dumped in the freezing ocean to drown. Harvey had dove in and rescued her.

"You already thanked me for that."

"You came back to us," she said. "I never thanked you for *that*."

"You know why I'm here?"

"In the team?"

"Yeah."

"Go on."

"Frank gave me a choice, either I stay and work in the team, or I go to prison."

"For what?"

"I boiled a man alive, Melody." Harvey looked across at her, and she nodded. She'd found the body with Frank. "Plus, doubtless Frank would heap on as many unsolved crimes as he could."

"So you're not here because you *want* to be here?" Melody was taken back.

"I wasn't, not at first." Harvey smiled. "I kind of like you guys, it's a big change for me, I never had people on my side like this before. It was always dog eat dog."

Melody moved away. "No, Harvey, it's wrong. You need to be with us one hundred percent. We're a team, we're all one hundred percent invested in this, and if one of us isn't then that person is putting the rest of our lives in danger."

"Hey, I'm here. I made the choice, didn't I?"

"It wasn't a particularly *hard* choice, was it? Let's face it."

"Yes, it was a hard choice, Melody. All my life, I've been hiding from people like us, people like Frank. How easy do you think it was to do this? But you know what, it's been a year now, and we're a damn good team. I like it here."

"So could you walk away right now?" asked Melody.

Harvey didn't reply.

"Frank still has you doesn't he?"

"He said he'd help," replied Harvey. "Frank won't take the noose off until all my questions are answered, and I can focus."

"What questions? You *found out* who raped your sister."

"My parents, I need to know who they were, why they were killed-"

"And who killed them?"

Harvey didn't reply.

"Jeez, Harvey, we all have questions, we don't all go around moping about them, you have to move on."

"When I have the answers, Frank will take the noose off."

"And *then* what?

"And then I get to choose, I guess."

"Between?"

"Freedom."

"And? Freedom and what, Harvey?"

"Boredom?"

Melody moved closer to him, "This is freedom to you?"

"I've given it a lot of thought, Melody."

"And?"

"I'm doing what I always did, what I'm good at. Only now I'm doing it for the good guys."

"Is that all?"

"No, I'm also doing it with people I like and respect.'

"Like friends?"

"I guess you could call it that. I've only ever had one friend, so I'm not one hundred percent sure."

"What happened to him?"

"He was killed,"

"Tell me about him."

"What can I say? Julios was the only one that was ever there for me. He was my foster father's bodyguard, then when Hannah died, he became my mentor, he trained me."

"Trained you to be a *killer*?"

"Yeah, but not at first. I was only twelve right, it wasn't a career move. But I was angry, he channelled my anger, taught me self-defence, aikido and all that. He helped me grieve."

"He showed you how to kill though?" asked Melody. "And not get caught."

"He showed me how to do many things, Melody."

"And you know who killed him?"

"I will do. If it takes me another twenty years, I won't stop, Melody. I'll find him just like I did the men who raped Hannah."

Melody was silent for moment. "So, if we're friends, tell me something. About *you* I mean. Something that doesn't involve killing."

"Like what?"

"Like where you live, where you go, what you do. You're a mysterious man, Harvey Stone, and we're, well we're a curious bunch. Maybe if we knew more about you, we could all be better friends?"

"This *is* what I do."

"And where do you go? At night I mean, where's home?"

"Not far."

"You're being coy," said Melody. "Okay, is there a potential Mrs Harvey Stone?" Melody smiled, she was enjoying watching Harvey be uncomfortable.

"Not really, women never really worked out for me, they asked too many questions they wouldn't like the answers to."

"You have your eye on anyone? I mean, come on, we all need an outlet right?"

"There's no-one, Melody."

"Okay, nice to know. Maybe I can set you up with one of my friends?"

"That won't be necessary, Melody."

"Okay, I can see this is making you uncomfortable, let's

leave it there, but I am going to learn you, Stone." She looked up at him. Harvey looked back. Then, over her shoulder, he saw a huge black plume of smoke erupting from the Isle of Dogs, which was visible just a few miles along the river. It was followed by the faint, dull thump of a distant explosion a few seconds later. The noise was deep and angry-sounding, rumbling towards them and beyond.

"What the-"

"Back inside, let's go," said Harvey.

They ran the hundred yards back to the building and walked inside. Denver was underneath the van, Reg was tapping away furiously on his computer keyboard, and Frank was nowhere to be seen.

"Reg," said Melody, "get me the satellite of the Isle of Dogs."

"Eh? What for-"

"Just get it up, there's been an explosion." She called upstairs, "Frank, you need to see this."

"See what?" he called from inside his office.

"Explosion. Isle of Dogs. It's a big one."

Frank stepped from his office and looked down. "How long?"

"One minute ago, Harvey and I saw it from the river."

"Looks like Canada Square, but the smoke's too thick to see where exactly," said Reg.

"Reg, get us a news broadcast, we may as well see what's happening."

In true Reg style, he dragged multiple news feeds across several of his screens, muted two of the channels and played the audio of one over the speakers. According to the presenter, a video had been sent in by a member the public who had captured the scene on his phone. Media teams were also in the area were setting up. All three of the separate news broadcasts showed breaking news at the bottom of the screen, and after a few minutes, live video feeds began to show what the team saw on the satellite imagery. Thick black smoke and people running from the buildings. A reporter on the scene stood amid the chaos of crowds, ambulances, police cars and fire engines, all working hard to evacuate the public and close off the area. A few teenagers could be seen taking videos on their mobile phones behind the reporter. Another news channel repeated the video footage from moments after the blast, sent into them by another member of the public. Smoke poured from the ground floor lobby of One Canada Square, an iconic tower in London's Canary Wharf.

Ten minutes had passed, and people were still emerging from the smoke-filled building. The reporter stopped talking to allow the cameraman to film the remaining workers walk away. Most came out coughing and ran past the firefighters who stood outside ready to douse any fires that emerged. The evacuated workers held shirts and rags up to their faces. A group of women held their shoes in their hands and ran along the street barefoot, directed by the police to an assembly point away from the building. The assembly point was down some steps in a small square beside the river. One man casually strode away, his coat and bag hung over one arm, in the other he held a small boy's hand tightly. The man was Asian, the boy was caucasian.

"That man there, watch that man," said Frank.

"What do you see?" asked Reg.

"The man with the boy. He's too casual, he looks out of place. He's not scared, plus look how he's clutching his bag and the boy's hand, he's heading for the kill zone."

"The what?"

"No, stop him," said Frank to the screen. "Reg get me someone on the scene. I can't be the only the only seeing this."

"Who do you want? The officer in charge?"

"No, his phone will be crazy, get me the Isle of Dogs fire department, quickly, Reg."

The phone rang over the speakers and, a few seconds later, a woman answered hurriedly. Frank spoke over her introduction. "Sorry, lady, this is DI Frank Carver from SO10, I understand your units are attending the blast in Canada Square?"

"Who are you? Yes, they are–"

"Good. Get hold of your officer in charge, there's a male IC6 currently walking from the scene towards the assembly point, and he's loaded. Do it now, you can make a note of this number and call back for confirmation of my credentials, but I urge you act quickly. We can iron out your questions later."

"This is most–"

"Lady, there's a man with a bomb in his bag walking towards the assembly point. Make the call."

"Disconnect the call, Reg."

Melody, Reg and Denver all looked across to Frank who stood transfixed, staring at the screens. "Stop him, come on, someone." He spoke to the screen as the suspect, just meters away from the reporter, remained within the camera-man's frame. Another broadcast showed a group of fire-fighters stood beside the truck. The team watched as one of the men took a call over his radio and began to look around.

"There's our man," said Frank. "He's spotted him." The firefighter shouted a uniformed policeman over to him and began pointing towards the suspect. A group of several hundred people had congregated in the assembly point five hundred yards from the building. The policeman immediately got on his radio, and another one appeared from the steps that led down to the assembly point. The policeman was small in the picture in the distance behind the reporter, but the team could easily see him emerge from the steps and hold his hand up to stop the suspect with the bag and the boy. He returned a call into his radio.

More people emerged from the building and ran towards the assembly point.

"No," said Frank. "Get away. For God's sake, take him down."

There seemed to be an argument between the cop and the suspect, who was indicating that he wanted to go down the steps to the assembly point. But the uniformed policeman blocked his path and was struggling to hear his commanding officer over his radio.

Then, without warning, the broadcast went bright white, immediately followed by a *Signal Lost* message across the screen.

The team were silent. Reg folded his arms over his head and rested it on his desk.

"Oh my god. Did we really just see that?" said Melody, her head in her hands.

Harvey and Denver stood silent.

Frank lowered his head, removed his glasses and rubbed the bridge of his nose. "Team, take as long as you need to digest what you just saw. We reconvene in the meeting room as soon as everyone is ready." Frank turned and walked up the mezzanine stairs to his office. Harvey watched him wipe his eyes as he closed the door.

The white screen was directed back to the news studio. Melody had walked backed to her desk to be alone. Reg held his face in his hands, and Denver and Harvey stood transfixed at the shocking news.

The news reporter began to talk with a broken and emotional voice. "We have just witnessed a tragedy. A cold-blooded attack on our nation's capital has just taken place. Ladies and gentlemen, a hotline is being set up for those who want to communicate with loved ones who may have been at the scene. We are still waiting for a damage report-"

"This is disgusting," said Denver. "I feel sick."

"It's cowardly," said Harvey. "I wish I could get my hands on the sick bastard."

"You and half the country, mate."

"I feel so helpless, stood here watching it on the news. We're supposed to be fighting this sort of thing."

"No mate, that's not us," said Denver. "We need to focus on what we're doing, we're not trained for this sort of thing." He paused. "How many do you think-"

"Killed?" asked Harvey. "Who can say? We'll find out soon enough. But what does it matter? If it's one or one hundred, it's still a loss, it's still an attack."

The news reporter broke the tension between the two men. "And this just in, the BBC have just received information from known terrorist, Faisal Al Sayan, claiming responsibility for the blast. He has made no threats, no demands." The screen showed a photo of a Middle-Eastern man in a white headscarf with a hooked nose and thick beard. The reporter continued. "The Afghani man, who is at large in the UK, has claimed the blast a victory that, in his own words, will send a message to the city. He claims he will cleanse London, and make it a beautiful, sinless place once more."

———

Frank waited patiently for the team to arrive, he allowed them time to sit and settle, then began.

"I think it's prudent to observe a one minute silence for those who were lost in the tragedy we all just witnessed.

The room was already silent and remained so for the minute's entirety.

"What we all just saw is truly the height of what we are up

against in modern day Britain. Such a cowardly attack is just one example of the war we are fighting. The people you saw congregated in the assembly area and running along the streets are those we serve to protect, those we are sworn to protect." The team nodded.

"However, this unit is *not trained* to fight the war on terrorism. There are others that are fighting that particular war. We fight alongside them, yes, and behind them, for sure." Frank took a deep breath and focused on each of the team individually.

"We are professionals, we *must* remain professional, and we must continue with our work as hard as it is in times like this. I *know* the urge to go and offer assistance is high, but *trust* me, *now* is the time we need to be vigilant. *Now* is the time that criminals attack, when all eyes are looking elsewhere. *Now* is the time that Al Sayan will be moving, planning, and preparing for a follow-up attack. But Al Sayan is not our concern, our target is Stimson. We *must* remain emotionally intelligent. *Do not* let the horrors that unfolded today obscure your vision. Or else we will lose this battle. Is that understood?"

The team nodded.

"I do *not* want any heroes. Is that clear?"

"Yes, sir," said Melody. Reg and Denver both grumbled a confirmation.

"Tenant?"

"Yes, sir," said Reg.

"Any questions?"

"No, sir."

"Good, well done, guys, get to it. I have every faith in you all."

7

SHADOW OF THE MONSTER

The mood was sombre as the team prepared.

Melody began loading the back of the van with her kit. She had Peli cases containing binoculars, a small tripod that held a sighting scope, and another for the DLSR camera, along with various lenses. Each item, including the binos, camera and scope, had the foam insert carefully cut out around it to ensure a snug fit.

Reg had given her a bag of tracking chips, which LUCY was able to pick up and communicate with once they were activated. Melody didn't intend on getting too close to Larson, but if the opportunity arose, she would slip a chip into his pocket or his car. The chips themselves were tiny, and if placed correctly, the carrier wouldn't even know they were there.

LUCY was an extremely powerful software and hardware combination that Reg had built and developed himself. Officially, LUCY stood for Location and Unilateral Communication Interface, which produced the acronym, LUCI. But Reg had given her the unofficial name of Lets Us Catch You, so she remained LUCY.

There had been no expense spared on the design and build of LUCY. The interface ran on a master server, which was water cooled, had twenty-four multicore processors and one hundred and twenty-eight gigabytes of memory. In addition to the master server, LUCY called upon the resources of three slave units with identical specs to the master. The software ran on a virtual operating system so that if at any point the master server crashed, a slave unit would step up and take its place.

LUCY's database was striped across several block-level storage systems, giving her a combined storage potential of one hundred and twenty-eight petabytes. The entire system was powered by four high-powered, uninterruptible power supplies and a backup generator.

The immense power and speed of the software merely provided the infrastructure for LUCY's interface. Her capabilities allowed Reg to link together various other pieces of software to provide a one-stop shop for satellite imagery to identify the location, speed, height above sea-level and temperature of digital trackers that could be placed anywhere. The chips were five millimetres square, which meant that they could be put in a mobile phone, items of clothing or even, as Reg had done to Harvey six months previously, hidden inside a watch.

In addition to the tracking of chips, LUCY could monitor mobile phones on virtually any network internationally. This allowed Reg to not only hear the conversations but access a live view of a smart phone's interface, which provided access to messages, calendars, contacts and more.

LUCY's primary function had been to monitor communications on suspects and monitor operatives' whereabouts. However, due to the success of the system, Reg had been granted an additional budget to enhance the system to include the security of the building, the comms system, and the digital telephone system. Reg had taken the upgrade to the next level and was able to control headquarters within headquarters. He could open and close the shutter doors, change the temperature, manage the alarm system and control the lighting. These additional features didn't provide any value to the unit, but made life easier for Reg.

Each of the team had various chips on their person at all times. Reg had installed them in their phones, in case the signal was ever lost, and in their vehicles and coats. Lucy was able to detect anomalies in behaviour and provide alerts. If a carrier had a habit of driving a particular route at a particular time of day, LUCY would alert Reg if they one day took a different route. He could set various thresholds per carrier to provide alerts should an operative veer off course by a given distance.

Denver wiped his tools and put them back in the relevant drawers inside his tool chests. He'd been doing maintenance on the van, which was brand new and needed little effort to upkeep, but it was what Denver did. It was Denver's responsibility to ensure that the vehicles were maintained and that routes were planned. If somebody needed an entry or extract, he would know the potential exit routes, times, speeds, and safe places to tuck themselves away. It was a far cry from his days as a teenager when he would be chased across the country in a stolen supercar. He'd been trained by the best, and although his defensive driving and tactical driving were impeccable, he knew the safest thing to do if being chased in a town is to hole up out of sight. Being in a car and trying to get away in the age of the internet was just asking for failure. Having several locations near to an extract, where he knew he could get out of the sight of satellites and the public eye, was key to a good exit strategy. Usually, when the chaos had died down, a slow drive out a city or town was safer than driving at over one hundred miles per hour trying to outrun someone, which would be like waving a flag to whoever is doing the chasing.

"Okay, guys, here's your location, I'm sending it across to your phones now. You're looking for a place called Wethersfield, about fifteen minutes from Braintree in Essex. I've got Larson, Stimson and our mystery man on screen, and I'll update you first thing if the location changes," said Reg.

"Thanks," said Melody. "You going to miss us, Reg?"

"While you guys are out on a joy ride, I'll be busting through World War Two on my new game."

"Is that right, Tenant?" said Frank from above him on the mezzanine.

Reg looked startled at Frank's voice above him. "Well, it's not precise, sir, but I'll be thinking about it."

"Mills, Stone, stay in touch with Tenant."

"Will do, sir," said Melody. "We set?" she said to Denver.

"We are, I'll drop you home then pick you up in the morning. Harvey, you want a ride home or you taking your bike? Looks like the weather's going to get awful nasty out there."

"I'll take my bike and meet you in Wethersfield, we might need two vehicles."

"Suit yourself, say six am?"

"I'll be there."

"Let's do it," said Denver, and he started up the van. He listened to the van's engine purr for a few seconds then climbed into the driver's seat. "Reg?"

Reg looked across the floor of the headquarters with his eyebrows raised.

"Door?" said Denver.

"I'm a doorman is what I am," said Reg, hitting a button on his keyboard. "An overqualified doorman," he called to Melody as her downcast face passed by, and Denver put his foot down. Harvey followed the van out on his bike and Reg hit the door button again, causing the sliding metal shutters to close.

The three news channels still showed the devastation of the bomb scene at Canary Wharf, but the sound was down. Reg switched them off.

"You don't want to know what's going on, Tenant?" said Frank from above.

Reg stayed looking at LUCY's interface on the screen in front of him. "It's not that I'm not interested, sir. It's just that we have a job to do, and as much as it pains me, going after Al Sayan is not part of that job. I'm not a violent man, sir, as you know, but I bet there isn't one Brit that wouldn't like to get his hands on that guy right now. I dread to think what would happen if Harvey got hold of him."

"Thankfully, Harvey won't have a chance."

"How did you know, sir?'

"Know what, Tenant?"

"About that man in the suit?"

Frank thought back to the horrific scene that had played out. "Do you know what a kill zone is?"

"I've heard it being talked about, but-"

"What happens when a bomb goes off, or a shooting takes place?"

"How do you mean?"

"Well, what would *you* do if you were in that situation?"

"I'd run I guess, I hope anyway."

"Exactly, and where would you run?"

"Away from the bomb or the shooter."

"Right. So a nasty, despicable, tactic that terrorists use is to create a second bomb in an area they know that people will congregate. For example, the emergency evacuation assembly point for Canada Square was that little flat area by the water, where the cameras were pointing. So once the first bomb had gone off on the ground floor, the bombers knew that the evacuation procedures would lead the workers all to that point. Simple. Send the second bomb to that point. There's a few hundred people, maybe more all huddled together."

"That's sick, sir."

"It's modern warfare I'm afraid."

"But how did you know it was him?"

"When all this is over, I'll play the recording back, you'll see for yourself. He had tell-tale signs."

"You've seen that kind of thing before?"

Frank hesitated. "Many times. Over and over, Tenant. Each time I watched the people all run to what they thought was safety."

"Sir?" said Reg. Frank was staring.

"Sorry." Frank roused himself. "God forbid you're ever in a situation like that, Tenant."

8

BEAST OF BURDEN

DENVER DROPPED MELODY HOME AND TOOK THE SHORT ride to his own home. He kept the music off, absorbed by his own thoughts of the images he'd seen that day. It wasn't the first terrorist attack he'd witnessed. He'd seen the reports of the 9/11 attacks in New York, and the subsequent 7/7 attacks in London. He even vaguely remembered the IRA attacks in London when he was younger, but that was the first time he'd actually seen the bomb go off. It was horrific. Lives had instantly been lost just as they had in other attacks, but witnessing the blast somehow made it more real. Maybe because technology was more efficient, it allowed the media to broadcast faster. Whatever it was, Denver had been hit hard. His eyes moistened as he drove. Sorrow, hate and all kinds of emotion consumed his mind.

It was late in the day when Denver arrived in Barking, Essex. He had a little two-bed house in front of a park. The ride to work was under thirty minutes, and the location was far enough out of town for him to feel away from it all. That day he felt closer than ever, but that was the job. He loved the team. He and Reg worked well together, and Melody was hard working, which pushed Denver to perform. Harvey had been difficult to get used to, but during the human trafficking case, Melody had been kidnapped and thrown into the sea, and Harvey and Denver had a few moments that brought them closer. Harvey was a good guy. He'd done some terrible things that Denver could never empathise with or even forgive, but it wasn't his place to judge. From what he'd seen so far, Harvey had a stronger moral compass than any of the team.

Denver stopped at the church at the top of the road. There was no service on, but Denver liked to sit in the quiet. He'd been misguided as a youngster and considered himself fortunate to have been set on a new path, a good path, with a career that allowed him to do good things. He was certain that if the opportunity hadn't arisen to join the force, he would be in prison by now. Reg had said once that maybe that's why Denver liked Harvey so much because they both had a background of crime. But Denver had argued that while he had graduated from stealing old Ford Capris and Escorts to high-end Ferraris and McClarens, Harvey had been immersed in a criminal world as a child and had killed his first man at twelve years old. It was a different league. There was no crossover.

A few people sat alone in the church pews. Candles lined the altar rails and cast weak shadows on the cold stone walls, lost in the gloom that hung above the wooden beams high above. Denver walked slowly and quietly to the front pew, where he sat and bowed his head. He wasn't devoutly religious, but his mother was, and an element of her religious spirit carried with him. It guided his morals, as a blind man might use a cane. When a blind man's cane hit something solid, the blind man would stop and feel around for the right way to go. When Denver found something that itched his sense of right and wrong, he'd stop and ask himself what his mother might do. It was his way of asking himself what God might do, but without directly being reliant on religion.

Aside from the morality guidance, Denver enjoyed the peace and harmony of the old church, which often sought following the horrors of his job. They were expected to be hardened to horrific scenes and evil people, and were asked to perform actions that crossed so many lines of morality. The church allowed Denver to reposition his actions; it cleansed him.

Denver lit a candle for those who had fallen earlier that day. He thought of their families and their suffering, although they would never know that, out there, a man unknown to them was grieving and sharing their pain. Denver left the church and drove the short distance home. After parking the van in his driveway, instead of going inside, he walked the one hundred yards to his local grocery store. The store was cheaper than supermarkets and more convenient for Denver's erratic routine. A small price to pay for the quality of life he led.

"Mr Denver, sir, how are you?" said Ali, the grocer.

"Mustn't grumble, Ali," said Denver. "How's the kids?"

"Oh, they're fine, they're upstairs playing on their video game. It's quieter down here I think. All those car races, explosions and guns, I sometimes wonder how they sleep."

Denver thought on that; it sounded like a typical day at work. "New generation Ali. Gone are the days of conkers and hopscotch." Denver was filling his basket with a small loaf of bread, avocados, bananas and spinach. He picked up a few tins of soup and some tea and walked to the counter. Ali emptied the basket and placed the items in a plastic bag.

"All in one bag, Ali, no need to separate them."

"Same every time, Mr Denver. "

"Save the planet, Ali." Denver smiled.

"It all helps. Is this on your account?"

"I'll settle at the end of the month?"

"That's fine, Mr Denver, your credit's good. Enjoy your evening."

"You too, Ali. Thanks." Denver walked out the store and heard the little bell above the door. He took a slow walk back to his house, locked the front door behind him and placed his bag in the kitchen. It was an old house built just after the Second World War, when babies were booming and industry had started to pick up again. The Ford factory less than two miles away had provided jobs for many of the local men. But in recent years, the British automobile industry had steadily declined, and the houses now provided homes for a vast variety of people and cultures.

Denver poured a tin of mushroom soup into a pan and set it to boil. While it cooked, he halved an avocado and scooped out the delicious fruit with a small spoon onto a plate.

His living room was small with a TV in one corner, a selection of DVDs on a shelf, and a large couch with a coffee table in front. There wasn't much room for any more furniture and Denver didn't need anything else. He rarely had visitors, unless he brought his mum home for Christmas, but typically he'd go to hers. Her house was more of a home than his own. He turned the TV on with the remote and found a nature documentary straight away. He didn't flick through the channels as he knew that many of them would be showing the day's horrors. Denver had quietened his mind, he didn't need reminding.

He sat on his couch and ate the soup, followed by the avocado, then set about washing his plates and the pan in the small kitchen sink. He placed the items on the drying rack where they lived. He rarely used anything else in the kitchen, and it was pointless putting them away each night.

He showered and dressed in tracksuit bottoms and an oversized t-shirt, then took the loaf of bread into the garden to scatter crumbs for the birds. His garden was small but stylish. There were no overhanging trees so there were no piles of leaves, just well-trimmed bushes and hardy plants. A small lawn area stood in the middle, and a little table with one chair sat by the back door. In the summer months, he'd drink his morning tea in the garden and watch the birds. The high walls around his property gave him all the seclusion he needed. It wasn't a perfect home, but it was his home, and it was as nice as he could get until retirement.

Denver dreamed of St Lucia, where his family home stood near long, perfect beaches that lined the turquoise ocean, heated by the incessant, golden sun. He'd travelled there before with his mum, when her own mum had died. He'd lain beneath palm trees on his grandfather's hammock with a book and enjoyed the tropical breeze. That's how he'd spend his final days. It was all he needed to drag him through the horrors of the modern world.

The nature show was still on when Denver sat back on the couch and heaved his legs up. He settled down with the remote on his chest and his phone by his side, then pulled a thick blanket over himself. He fell asleep to the soothing voice of David Attenborough and woke to the harsh shrill of his phone's ringtone.

"Harvey? What's up? It's late."

"I have a problem."

———

Harvey pulled into the driveway of his house in Buckhurst Hill. It was a rental. He only owned one property, and that was in the south of France. He'd owned it for a year and had only spent a few nights there when Frank had caught up with him and put the noose around his neck.

The little house in Buckhurst Hill was enough for Harvey.

Frank had the rent covered, but Harvey had to pay the bills. It was a good deal, all things considered.

He clicked the button on the electric garage door that he'd had fitted himself, and watched it open. He never left his bike outside the house for a number of reasons. Firstly, he'd grown up in Theydon Bois not far from Buckhurst Hill, and knew that the affluent London suburbs were a target for small criminals from less affluent areas. Harvey had been on the wrong side of the law his entire life and had seen the people that openly spoke about heading out to Buckhurst Hill, Ongar, or Theydon Bois for a quick buck. They'd spend a few days sitting and watching then, when they knew the owner's habits, they'd empty the house. Not violent criminals, but heartless bastards who destroyed memories. Secondly, Harvey had had his bike for nearly ten years. He'd done enough jobs with it for anybody who was anybody in the organised crime world to know that the silver BMW belonged to the infamous Harvey Stone. Harvey didn't want those types of people knowing where he lived.

He rolled the bike in and clicked the garage door closed, then put his helmet in its protective bag and hung it from a hook. The garage was bare except for the bike and a rack of three hooks fixed to the wall beside the door into the house.

The house itself was built in the 1930s. It was solid brick with a bay window to one side of the front door, which a person could sit on and watch the world go by. A large chimney breast and fireplace was the feature of the lounge. The house had originally been one much larger house, but an opportunistic landlord had split it into two properties some years back.

Harvey had chosen the house because he was familiar with the area, and it was only twenty-five minutes to headquarters on his bike. Frank had suggested an apartment closer to headquarters, but Harvey preferred to live in a building with a ground floor. He could defend himself more easily in a house than in an apartment with only one exit.

The house was old and cold, but Harvey seldom used the heating system. He kept his jacket on and sat at the island counter in the kitchen on a bar stool. His Macbook was the only sign of modern technology in the house. The lounge had no TV, just a single armchair and a sofa he'd bought more to fill the empty space than to sit on. He slept in the armchair frequently.

Harvey had many nights where his mind would go over and over the facts surrounding his parents. He'd sit in the armchair in the darkness, his mind a whirl of possibilities. One day, he knew that one of those possibilities would be plausible, and he'd be able to delve deeper. But for now, his only knowledge of his parents was the cock and bull story his foster father had told him, verbatim, for close to thirty years.

Harvey pictured John telling him the story with a tumbler of brandy in his hand. Three ice cubes chinked to the side of the glass as John recalled his fable to repeat it once more.

"We only had one bar back then, we did things ourselves, your mum and me. We served drinks ourselves if the barmaids were off, we put orders into the brewery, and we even cleaned the bar at close up. That was when we found you both. You in a little picnic hamper wrapped in blankets with a note. Hannah sat beside you, wide-eyed and scared."

The note had said that Harvey's parents had killed themselves; life had got too much for them. John and Barb had fostered Hannah and her baby brother, Harvey.

Harvey had been researching his birth parents, based on John's story, for as long as could remember. There were no records of anybody named Stone in Plaistow, where the alleged bar had been, not that matched the ages that Harvey's parents would have been anyway. There was no record of a single suicide in the area at the time, let alone a double suicide. There were no marriage records, no mortgages, not anything that pointed to something of any use. The only consistent thing Harvey had discovered was the story that John had told him time and time again.

Harvey opened his laptop and stared at the little box in the search engine. It was as empty as the results it would produce. He closed the lid without typing anything and rested his head in his hands.

His mind wandered to the blast they'd seen earlier that day. It had been shocking, disturbing even. Harvey was a ruthless killer. He'd done things to people that would make most people vomit with disgust. But even he was hit hard by the images they'd seen that day. It was so much worse because they'd seen the killer walking nonchalantly towards the huddle of innocent people.

Perhaps that was it, perhaps that was why Harvey was disgusted. He'd always stood up for the weak and innocent. He'd always preyed on cowardly bullies that ruined peoples lives. During the time that he worked for his foster father, he and Julios had been hitmen. They'd done things that required a certain skill set and a very specific mindset. Things that John's other men could have done, but they would have been messy, and brought retaliation to the family's operations.

It was during Harvey's time as a hitman that he'd taken on training, in preparation for the day when he met his sister's rapist. He would scour the news for early releases or arrests of sex offenders, rapists or molesters, and target them. He honed his skills on the bullies. He would track them, watch them and learn them, then plan their suffering and execute his plan with brutal force. He'd seen many a man suffer, and watched them as they fell from the lofty heights of self-assurance to weak, soiled and pitiful victims. They all cried, all thirty-three of them. They all pissed themselves in fear. They all died a prolonged and agonising death.

Harvey couldn't shake the image of Al Sayan from his mind. Crimes such as robbing a priceless buddha were not harmful to anybody. In another life, Harvey would let Stimson do what he wanted, it was no skin off his nose, nobody was hurt. But when victims' lives are ruined, and pain and suffering are brought upon the weak and helpless, Harvey couldn't help but feel the anger inside him grow. Yet the politics surrounding the good side of the law placed Al Sayan in the jurisdiction of some other team.

Harvey moved from his kitchen to his lounge and fell into the soft armchair. He put his feet up on a soft footstool and linked his fingers on his stomach. He sat for a while, and tried to steer his thoughts towards his parents. What might they look like? How old would they be? What did his father do for work? But each time, his mind took a U-turn and brought him back to the photo news broadcasts had shown; the bearded, unsmiling face of Al Sayan.

Peace wasn't ready for Harvey that evening. His mind raced with the blast, the beard, the crooked nose, and, of course, his parents. He decided instead to go for a run to try and clear his mind of everything. He changed into shorts and a hooded sweater and started with a slow jog from his door. Harvey ran every morning except when he was on an all-nighter with work. He never ran the same route, a lesson he'd learned from Julios.

Epping forest was once a vast area that covered much of the county, but was now reduced to a few miles of woodland. In Buckhurst Hill, it was still a great place to run. Harvey followed no trails, he just ran where his feet took him. He hurdled fallen trees and streams and sprinted up hills. By the time he was finished, he'd run six miles, and warmed down by walking the last two hundred yards from the end of his street to his house. It was a quiet night.

He closed the front door behind him and slid the bolt

across, an old habit, then kicked off his running shoes and walked up the stairs. He reached behind the shower curtain and turned the shower on; it usually took a few minutes to get hot. Then he stepped into his bedroom, which was the smaller of the two rooms at the back of the house. He preferred it; the view of the forest was calming and familiar, and there was less chance of people looking in.

He stripped off his sweaty clothes and strode naked to the bathroom. Steam clouded from inside the shower, and the mirror was already beginning to fog. He slid the shower curtain back, looked down and stopped at what he saw.

Harvey turned the shower off, quietly stepped back to his bedroom and retrieved his Sig. He swept the house, checked the spare room then ventured downstairs. There was no sign or trace of anybody. The front and back doors were locked with no signs of forced entry, as were the windows.

Harvey crept back up the stairs and dressed in clean cargo pants and a plain white t-shirt. He picked up his phone and dialled Denver's number from memory.

"Harvey?" said Denver. "What's up? It's late."

"I have a problem."

9

KNOCK KNOCK

AT FOUR AM, DENVER AND MELODY STOOD IN HARVEY'S bathroom looking down at the dead body that lay in the bathtub.

The man had been in his fifties by the look of his grey hair and the paunch that protruded from his midriff. He wore a pair of cheap running shoes, blue jeans and a dark grey cardigan over a checked shirt.

Two small dents in the bridge of his nose suggested he'd worn glasses, which may have been lost during his attack. A laminated identify card hung around his neck stating that Arthur Bell worked for Hackney Carriages as a black taxi driver. The card gave Arthur's driver number and showed a photo of the man much like a passport photo.

Harvey stood in his kitchen and watched Melody and Denver walk down the stairs to join him. Melody picked up the coffee she'd walked in with and leaned against the kitchen counter holding the cardboard cup in both hands.

"I'm guessing you don't know him?" she asked.

Harvey didn't reply.

"It's a bit random isn't it?" said Denver. "I mean, what the hell?"

"Well it's not the first time you found a dead body in the bath," Melody said to Harvey. She was referring to the Sergio incident when Harvey had boiled his sister's rapist alive. "Sorry, that was uncalled for."

Harvey didn't reply. He had learned from his training with Julios a method of communicating without words. A look, a gesture, or sometimes no response at all could express his thoughts.

"Shall we tell Frank?" asked Melody, moving the conversation along. "We need to get the body out of here."

"I don't see what Frank would do," said Denver, "except call the police, and have it dealt with the same as any other murder. Then Harvey will be arrested and out of action until he clears his name."

Harvey looked up at Denver.

"Let's get Reg on it," said Melody. "He can do some research on Arthur Bell for us. Find out who he is, his history, and probably even the last fare he had."

Just then, there was a hard knock on the door, three taps. Denver and Melody looked at Harvey, who put his finger to his lips and crept toward the door. He looked through the spy hole and edged back to the kitchen.

"Police. I'm being set up. Back door, quick." Harvey picked up the rucksack he'd packed the previous night and quietly opened the back door. They stepped out into the dark morning. The sun was still way below the horizon and the trees from the forest cast a gloom over the long, narrow garden. There was no side entrance to the house so any police looking to cover the rear would have to walk to the end of the street and find their way along the fence in the forest.

Harvey peered over the fence into the trees. He saw no movement, so quietly opened the back gate and let Melody and Denver out. As he closed it, he heard the sounds of the front door being forced in. Lights came on in the house.

Harvey led his two colleagues into the forest and took a wide circle back to the high street, five hundred yards from the entrance to his road. Once clear of the house, the three walked like they were walking off a Sunday roast. Melody cradled her coffee, Denver strolled with his hands in his pockets, and Harvey walked calmly and quietly. They reached the tree line where the forest met the main road.

"Denver, *tell* me you didn't park the van directly outside my house?"

"Give me *some* credit, Harvey. It's parked on the main road. We walked the five hundred yards down to yours."

"Okay, Melody and I will wait here in the tree line. You want to grab the van and get us? If I'm being framed for murder, then my face will be on the minds of every cop around here."

"Sure," I'll take a look down your road and see what's happening too."

"I can tell you what's happening, Denver. Uniformed police have found Arthur Bell, have called in the brain squad to deal with the body, and also put a call out to all units to be on the lookout for an IC1 male that fits my description."

"At least it solves your problem," said Melody.

Harvey looked across at her.

"You don't need to worry about getting rid of the body anymore." She smiled apologetically.

"Is the house clean?" asked Denver.

"Yeah, of course," said Harvey. "Everything I own is here apart from my bike." He gestured with his thumb to the backpack. "I can't go back there. I'll need to find somewhere else, at least until we find out who did this."

"Right, sit tight, guys, I'll be a few minutes," said Denver and strode out of the forest. He looked both ways then walked towards the van.

"To work out who did it, we need to understand why they did it," said Melody. "Any old enemies?"

"How many fingers you got?"

"Okay, are there any old enemies that you have seen or been in contact with recently?"

"None, I cut free of all that. The only thing I've done recently that links me to anything is what I've done for Frank and you guys. And we-"

"Yeah, we locked everyone up who you didn't kill," said Melody straight-faced.

"I don't think it's that," said Harvey. "Someone's getting me out of the picture."

"And framing you in another?"

Harvey didn't reply.

"But what's framing you for a murder going to achieve?"

"Is Reg online?"

"Bit early for him, he'll be there in about half hour." Why?"

"We need his research skills."

Denver pulled over to the side of the road beside the trees. He checked in front and behind then gave them the all clear. Melody and Harvey walked out of the trees. Melody climbed into the passenger seat, and Harvey laid down in the back of the van out of sight.

"Cheers, Denver, let's go, mate. Let's get out of here before they shut the place down."

Denver indicated and pulled off into the empty road. The houses opposite Harvey's road behind them flashed blue every second. Harvey imagined the road chock-a-block with police cars. The neighbours would be at their windows. Discretion was not on the MET's priority list when it came to murder.

"Good morning sunshines." Reg's voice came across the radio. "How are we on this splendid day at such a fine hour?"

Melody picked up the handset and looked back at Harvey who shook his head.

"Is Frank there yet?" asked Harvey.

"And good morning to you, Reggie, you're bright and breezy this morning," said Melody over the handset.

"Well it's nearly five am, and I'm sitting at my desk alone in the dark. If I don't keep myself happy, I'll happily fall back to sleep."

"No Frank yet?" she asked.

"No, he said he'd be in later, said he'd give us time to get some results."

"That's kind of him. Listen, Reg." Melody turned back to Harvey, who nodded and held up his thumb and first finger, indicating that she tell Reg only what he needed to know. "We need you to look something up for us, but hey it's only a stab in the dark, so keep this one on the down low."

"Wow, early morning mysteries, what you got?"

"If I gave you the registration number of a black cab driver, could you do some digging? We're still about an hour from the manor house."

"Yeah, I'll see what I can find. Is that it? It's a bit vague."

"Right now that's all we have, Reg."

"Okay, you going to let me in on how you came about the number or why you want me to do this?"

"Yes, we will do, Reg, of course, but right now I need you see what you can get with an open mind. When you get back to us, we'll fill you in."

"I see, out of sight out of mind," said Reg, slightly deflated.

"Reggie, come on, I just want that brilliant mind of yours to not be obscured by details. I want to see what you can find. What do you say? Thirty minutes?"

"You know how to get me going, Melody. Righto, thirty minutes it is."

"Thanks, Reg, we love you," said Melody and put the handset down.

Once they were out of Buckhurst Hill, Harvey sat up and leaned against the side of the van on the wooden panelling behind Melody. The side behind Denver was home to Reg's workbench. Two computers were fixed down beneath it and two large screens sat atop the surface with a single keyboard and mouse.

A single cable ran up to the van's ceiling and out through a grommet that Denver had drilled into place. A motorised aerial increased the effectiveness of the van's radio comms with headquarters. A small, hidden transponder and receiver spoke to the satellites, allowing Reg access to the internet from virtually anywhere. But without Reg in the van, the whole workbench and associated electronics were useless.

Harvey felt the van's speed increase and knew that Denver had just pulled onto the A12, a busy four-lane motorway that ran from East London to the East Coast. Braintree was about thirty to forty minutes up the A12, so Harvey settled in and closed his eyes. He didn't know when the next sleep was coming.

10

MONSTER OF DEPRAVITY

"Did you see our little martyr?" asked Al Sayan into the phone.

"You sick bastard-"

"Now, now. You are forgetting yourself," replied Al Sayan. "How are your plans coming on?"

"You'll get what you want, just don't touch my-"

"Your little Angel?" asked Al Sayan. "Now that you have seen how serious I am, I hope you will apply the same level of professionalism to the job as you would any other job. The stakes are high."

"And Stone? You said he was running. What from?"

"I imagine right about now he's being locked in a cell where he belongs," said Al Sayan. "But he is a troublesome fellow, so I urge you to take precaution. You have less than two days. What are you doing now?"

"I'll run my own job. I don't need your help, it's better that way."

"Good, I'd hate to see Stone come between you and your daughter, so do tell me if you need assistance. I have men who would gladly give their lives to take the nuisance down and allow me to carry out my own plans."

"I told you I don't need your help."

"Good, so you don't need me to tell you that all of your phones are being monitored by Stone's team. They are watching your every move. I'll leave you to deal with that shall I?"

Silence.

"I shall contact you again before the deadline is up."

"Wait."

There was a pause.

"I'm here," said Al Sayan.

"Let me talk to her."

"I told you before that you do not call the shots. I can assure you she is safe with me. The next time you talk to her will be in one of two potential circumstances. One, you have achieved your goal and delivered to me what I have requested."

"You'll get it."

"Two, little Angel will be trundling out of here with a little surprise in her cute little pink backpack."

"I need proof of life."

Al Sayan was silent for a moment. "Send your man to me, Mr Larson. Send him to my garage in Stratford. He will be followed, no doubt. He will see how well I am caring for Angel, and I will make sure the pests are eliminated."

11

MONSTER'S MANOR

"WE'RE COMING INTO WETHERSFIELD NOW," HARVEY heard Denver say. He opened his eyes and rubbed his face.

"We have water?" Harvey asked.

A bottle of water appeared over Melody's shoulder which he took, drank and returned.

"So what your game plan?"

"Reg, you there?" Melody called over the radio.

"Of course I am."

"Okay, give us some news, buddy."

"Arthur Bell. Fifty-two years old, married with two grown children. Lives in Slough, west of London. No previous record, same for his wife and kids."

The team were silent for a moment.

"So he's basically lived an average life?" asked Melody.

"Yeah, sounds about right."

"So why would somebody kill him?" asked Denver.

"For his taxi," said Harvey. "Whoever did it needs his taxi for something."

"Reg did you-"

"Check his taxi? Yeah of course. It was re-registered and

tested two months ago at Hackney Carriages, hasn't picked up any speeding tickets and has the GPS switched off."

"Reg?" said Denver.

"Go ahead, Denver."

"We're coming into Wethersfield now, can you give us a sitrep on Larson?"

"He and the mystery man are at the Manor House Hotel already, looks like they stayed in the hotel as they haven't moved since nine pm last night."

"Thanks, Reg," said Melody. She turned to Denver and Harvey, "how would you guys like to get some breakfast in the manor house?"

"Oh breakfast, come to me, baby," said Denver.

Harvey was on one knee between Melody and Denver's seats as they turned into the manor house's long driveway. Frank had been right, the surrounding landscape was only fields. The sun was rising somewhere behind a wall of grey but shone enough light for Harvey to see that escaping from the place would be difficult, especially if helicopters were in the air. There were no other buildings nearby, and no other streets for miles around.

Harvey leaned forward and picked up the handset. "Reg, Harvey."

"Go ahead, Harvey."

"Send us through any details of Larson's car, and Stimson's if you have it."

"Will do, it's coming at you now."

Harvey's phone beeped an incoming message. "Larson drives a black BMW seven series." He read the plate number out.

"Hey, Reg," said Melody, "we're going into the hotel side of the house for breakfast, see what we can see, keep your eyes on Larson and tell us if they move. We're hoping to catch them at breakfast and slip them a chip."

"Will do, you want to do a comms check?"

"Will the ear-pieces work this far out of London?" asked Melody.

"Should do, I beefed up the transmitter in the van. As long as you stay in range of it, the comms should be okay."

"What's the range?" asked Melody.

"Don't go more than five hundred yards away, the closer the better obviously."

"Gotcha, thanks, Reg," said Melody. She pushed the button on her ear-piece. "Reg, come back."

"Loud and clear," said Reg.

Melody looked at Denver and Harvey, they all nodded, confirming that they'd heard him. "Yeah, copy that, we're parking now."

"Just a heads up," said Reg, "I can see Larson and Stimson's minder in the hotel.

"Thanks, Reg."

"Black BMW seven series, first row of cars, near the door," said Denver.

"Melody, you have some of them chips on you?" asked Harvey.

"Yeah, Reg gave me a bag."

"Good, first chance we get we'll chip the BMW."

The team were greeted at the door of the manor house by a well-mannered man in a very stylish three piece suit.

"Good morning, welcome to Cornish House. Are you here for breakfast?" he said.

"We are," said Melody.

"If you'd care to follow me, then," he said and headed towards a set of large double doors, which he opened ceremoniously, and stood to one side. Melody followed close behind him, and Harvey and Denver tried their best not to look out of place.

As soon as the doors opened, Harvey scanned the room

for Larson. He spotted him at a table with a lady and a large man at the back of the massive room, away from the windows.

"Are there others joining your party, ma'am?" the man asked Melody.

"No, just us, thanks," she replied.

"I'll hand you to our concierge, and I hope you have a pleasant breakfast." He gave a small, discreet bow, turned and left through the double doors. Another man in an identical suit as the first man's greeted them. "Good morning. Do you have a reservation?" he asked.

"No, we don't know–"

"That's perfectly fine, I have a table for you over by the window just there, if you'd allow me to show you?"

"Can I ask where the washroom is?" asked Harvey.

"The washroom, sir?" the man said. "Yes, not at all, through the double doors at the back of the room. You'll also find shower facilities and our spa."

"That's great, do you think we could sit closer to the doors?" said Harvey.

"He's not feeling well," said Melody, "Are you dear?" Melody rubbed Harvey's back.

"No, I'm not feeling great." Harvey agreed.

"Perhaps then I might suggest another table. Please do follow me." The man turned and walked away, and the team followed. They reached a table for four, twenty yards from Larson and his company. The man offered Harvey a seat, but Harvey chose his own, one with an optimum view of Larson. Melody sat beside him, and Denver sat opposite with his back to the targets.

"I shall ask a waiter to join you shortly, please do have a nice breakfast, and I do hope you feel better, sir."

"Thank you, that's very kind," said Melody.

"That's Larson and Stimson's minder," said Harvey under his breath.

"Who's the woman?" asked Melody.

"Not sure," said Harvey. "We need ears over there."

The woman sat at the end of the table. Larson was to her right facing the team, and the minder sat opposite him. His broad shoulders covered most of Harvey's view, but Larson was easily recognisable from the photo Reg had provided.

"Okay first things first, let's get the car chipped. Then we'll work on getting a bug closer to Larson's table," said Melody.

"You have audio bugs?" asked Denver.

"Of course, we have these new ones that Reg gave me. Apparently, he can pick up the audio through LUCY, as long as they are in range of the van," said Melody.

"Can I take one?"

Melody passed him one.

"And a chip?"

She passed him a chip. "What are you doing?"

"Taking care of the car." Denver pushed his chair back. "Order me the full English, will you?" He left the room.

Harvey and Melody sat looking at the menu until a waitress approached them.

"Good morning, how are you both today?" she said.

"We're very well, thank you."

"Are you ready to order or would you care for more time?"

"We'll take three coffees, a full English for our friend, and I'll take the healthy omelette. What would you like, dear?" Melody said with a smile.

"Just coffee is good for me, thanks," said Harvey and handed the waitress the menu.

The waitress collected the other two menus. "I'll be back with the coffees shortly." She smiled and left.

Harvey casually glanced around the room as anybody might in a nice restaurant. He looked behind him, noted the paintings on the wall, and made a show of pointing to one and talking to Melody about it. Long emerald green curtains were tied back with braided gold rope onto elegant hooks and fixed into the walls. As Harvey's eyes made their way back to face forward, they fell on Larson, who stared unabashedly at him. He gave a half smile, blinked and turned his attention back to the woman.

Harvey did the same, turning back to Melody. He put his arm on the back of her chair, as a husband might do, and pulled his right leg up onto his left knee. He feigned talking to her about what they might do that day. Reaching across her, he pulled a tourist leaflet from a little stand at the end of the table. As he leaned over, he uttered under his breath, "I think it's a trap."

Melody said nothing but leaned into him to look at the leaflet, which described a tour of the manor house revealing its history and impressive art collection. The pamphlet was tri-folded, and the inside page was dedicated to the house's fantastic collection of artwork.

Harvey made a point of skipping past the pictures of the art and glanced at the rear page of the pamphlet before discarding it on the table as if he wasn't interested.

"What have you two lovebirds been talking about then?"

Harvey realised his arm was still on the back of Melody's chair. "Just playing the game, Denver," Harvey said quietly. "You all done?"

"Yeah, the chip's in the boot and the bugs are in the front under the dash," muttered Denver. He glanced around him. "Did you order yet?"

"Yeah, it's on its way," said Melody, just as the waitress reappeared with three coffees and a small silver bowl of sugar. The three cups of coffee each had a little shortbread biscuit on the saucer beside the cup, which sat on a white frilly dolly.

"Your order will be five minutes," said the waitress. "Can I offer you some toast and jam perhaps?"

"No, thank you," said Melody. "That'll be fine."

The waitress left.

A few minutes passed, then the waitress reappeared with another waiter pushing a small stainless steel cart. There were two large silver covers over the plates of food. They served the plates smoothly on the table in front of Melody and Denver.

"Can I get you anything else?" she asked.

"No, this is perfect, thank you very much," said Melody.

"You're welcome, please do enjoy your breakfast." The waitress and the waiter left, and Denver began to cover his breakfast in salt and ketchup. Harvey drank his black coffee and kept an eye of Larson with infrequent flicks of his eye.

Denver was halfway through his breakfast when Larson, the woman and the big guy stood. They thanked the waitress and left the table, walking behind Harvey and the team towards the exit.

"Okay, Reg are you hearing me?" said Melody.

"Loud and clear, Melody."

"Larson is on the move, he's with a woman and the minder. Are you able to identify the woman somehow?"

"I can't see any activity unless I know the number or the person's name."

"Where's Stimson, Reg?"

"Hold on, I'm just checking. He's way out, in Shepton Mallet," said Reg.

"Shepton Mallet? What's there?" asked Melody.

"A prison outside of Bristol," said Harvey. "But Stimson's a West Country guy right?"

"Yeah originally, he moves about a bit."

"Okay maybe he has a house there. Let's see if we can get a lead on the woman, Denver's chipped and bugged the

BMW. We're heading out now, we'll hang behind, and you can be our eyes, Reg."

"Copy that," said Reg.

Melody paid the bill as Denver and Harvey left and stood by the front doors. They saw the big guy climb into the black BMW. The woman opened the passenger door of a little Porsche, and Larson climbed into an Audi. The Porsche pulled off and drove slowly up the long driveway. The Audi followed, and the BMW pulled out behind the other two, obscuring the plates of the cars in front.

"That didn't work out, did it?" said Denver. "Reg, they've taken three cars."

"Okay, I can see Larson on the move, the minder guy is also moving," said Reg.

"Yeah, they all climbed into different cars. We're going to need to rely on Larson's phone to follow him. Keep on him Reg, we'll be on the road in one minute," said Harvey. Denver ran across to the van and started it up. By the time Melody came out the restaurant, Denver was at the bottom of the twelve grand steps that led from the main doors to the gravel driveway. She climbed in, and Denver put his foot down.

"So we're following Larson only. The other two are of no interest to us at this point, Reg."

"Copy, I've got Larson's phone up on LUCY. He's moved ahead of the other guy, looks like he's heading into London. The other guy is following him, but much slower."

"I knew it," said Harvey. "They spotted us in the restaurant. If we try to follow Larson, the big fella will step in."

"They spotted us?" asked Denver.

"Yeah, they recognised me somehow," said Harvey. "Hang behind the BMW, let's see where this goes."

"I don't see how they would recognise us," said Melody. "Surely-"

"He recognised *me*. Larson locked eyes with me, and it was more than a casual glance. He *knows* something."

"You think Arthur Bell?'

"That's exactly what I'm thinking."

Just then, the familiar sound of a police car's siren came in two short bursts from behind the van. Harvey looked out the back window and saw the roof of the police Volvo behind them.

"Ah, you must be kidding," said Denver.

"I'm guessing this isn't a tug for a driving offence, Denver," said Harvey. "Melody, if they take me away, get Frank on the case, but carry on after Larson."

"You sure?"

"Positive," Harvey replied. "You guys don't need to be wrapped up in this."

Denver came to a stop on the shoulder of the busy A-road and stepped out the vehicle. Harvey had his hand on the handle of the sliding door but held it closed. He waited to hear the police officer speak, but Denver spoke first.

"Morning, officer, how can I help?" said Denver politely.

"Place your hands on the vehicle please, sir."

"Excuse me?"

"Place your hands on the vehicle."

Denver leaned up against the van, and the police officer performed a search of his body. Denver didn't carry his issued weapon, but it was tucked under the seat in a fixed holster, ready to pull at a moments notice. A quick search of the van would raise some difficult questions.

"You might want to check my ID, officer, it's around my neck."

"All in good time, sir," the officer replied. He took his time searching Denver, feeling behind his belt, in his pockets, in the seams of his jacket, his shoes and socks.

"Aren't you supposed to tell me what it is I've done?" said Denver.

"Can you place your hands behind your back please, sir?"

"What? What for?" said Denver, he was getting annoyed.

"Just place your hands behind your back, so I can perform a search of the passengers," said the officer. His tone was flat and calm. He pulled the cuffs tight on Denver's wrists.

Melody stepped out the van. "Excuse me, sir, I think you're making a mistake." She held up her ID and stepped towards the officer, who twisted her arm back and slammed up her up against the van.

"What the hell are you doing?" cried Denver. "She's a cop for God's sake."

Harvey slid the door open and stepped out. "Stop, it's me you want." Harvey put his hands up. "Let her go, officer."

The police officer stepped back but held onto Melody's wrists. He slid the cuffs on and let her go. "Stand there," he told her and pointed to a spot beside Denver.

"Harvey Stone?"

"That's me."

"Hands on the vehicle." The officer gestured with his head to the van.

Harvey turned to the van and placed his hands high on the roof. The officer stepped behind Harvey, pulling another set of cuffs from his waist belt.

"Put your left hand only behind your back. That's your left hand only. Now."

Harvey brought his left hand down and allowed the police officer to fix one side of the cuffs to it. Harvey watched him in the reflection of the van's side window. The officer looked up to his right hand.

"Okay, now your-"

Harvey drove his right elbow back into the man's face, smashing the officer's nose. Before the man had a chance to react, Harvey grabbed onto the officer's neck and slammed his face into the van three times. Then he let the unconscious man fall to the ground.

"What the hell are you doing?" cried Denver.

"Harvey, you can't-" said Melody.

"He's either bent or a fake, my money's on him being fake," said Harvey.

"What makes you say that? You just beat up a police officer for God's sake, I'm not sure even Frank can help you there," said Melody.

Harvey bent down and emptied the policeman's pockets. He pulled the keys from the imposter's belt and uncuffed his colleagues.

"Denver, check the boot of that car will you?"

Denver walked to the police Volvo and opened the boot.

"You're not going to believe this," said Denver.

Melody walked over to join him.

"Is he alive?" asked Harvey, already knowing what they'd found.

"Yeah, he has a pulse," said Melody.

"Injured?"

"No. Drugged or knocked out by the look of it, but there's no blood or sign of injury anyway."

"Well, get him out of the car, people might notice a black guy and a girl standing here with a cop in the boot of his own police car."

Denver pulled the unconscious policeman up and lowered him to the floor, sitting him up against the side of the Volvo.

Harvey put the cuffs on the fake cop, opened the passenger door and ripped out the camera. He then found the hard drive storage unit it was connected to and ripped that out too.

He lifted the radio handset from the dash. "Officer down, officer down, three miles out of Braintree on the A131, assistance needed." He replaced the handset. "Let's go," he said to the others. Harvey climbed into the van and sat back down, putting the dash cam and hard drive on the floor beside him. "Now, people, let's move."

Melody and Denver walked back to the van, and within five minutes they were clear of the scene and on a back road heading towards the A12 into London.

"What the hell just happened there?" asked Denver.

"Fake cop, two objectives," said Harvey, "delay us, and take me out of the game."

"Reg, you there?" said Melody.

"I'm here, I heard it all. Everybody okay?" replied Reg.

"We're all good," said Harvey. "I'm going to call your number from the fake cop's phone, tell me what you know about it." Harvey dialled Reg's number.

Reg's phone lit up. "Okay, I have it, give me a sec."

"You still haven't told us how you knew he was a fake," said Melody.

"He didn't give a reason for tugging us, he was too rough with Denver and then you, then when he knew my name and didn't call for assistance, I knew it had to be fake. I'm wanted for Arthur Bell's murder right now. What policeman is going to try to arrest me and two other suspects on his own? Besides that, what policeman carries three sets of handcuffs unless they know they are going to be cuffing three people?"

"Okay I have it," said Reg over the comms. "It's a burner, but the call history is interesting."

"One of Stimson's?" asked Harvey.

"Without a doubt," confirmed Reg.

"Thanks, Reg. What's the update on Larson?"

"He's on the A12 heading into London, he's five miles out."

"Is Frank in yet?" asked Harvey.

"Not yet,"

"Good, how do I turn all this stuff on?"

"What stuff?" asked Reg.

"The computers in the back of the van. There's two computers, and I have a hard drive I want you to access."

"Power up the one on the left, and plug the drive into the USB port on the front."

Harvey leaned across and did as instructed. "Done."

"Okay, sit tight, I'll need a few minutes to access the computer over the satellite link," said Reg.

"Okay we need a sitrep," said Melody. "Frank sent us out to confirm Larson's location and do a recce on the manor house, and so far Harvey's wanted for a murder he didn't do, Larson has met with an unknown woman plus Stimson's bodyguard, and now the woman has disappeared and Larson and the goon are heading into London. Not a great report, even by our standards."

"Someone wants me out of the game," said Harvey. "They tried to frame me for murder, then tried to kill me."

"Kill you?" said Melody.

"Harvey leaned over into the passenger seat. "He was carrying this." He handed her a Glock handgun.

"He's not linked to the forces then," said Melody. "They wouldn't use this plastic crap,"

"Reg, it's Harvey."

"Go ahead."

"How many chips are on me right now?" Reg was known for planting hidden chips on the team so that Frank could see where they were at all times. Frank had asked Reg to plant as many as possible on Harvey, who had a habit of finding them and throwing them onto buses or into the handbags of passing women. There was nothing malicious meant by it, it was just Harvey's way of rejecting the noose around his neck.

"Five, Harvey," said Reg, like he was admitting he had a drinking problem.

"Five?" said Harvey, incredulous.

"Five. Your phone, your jacket, your shoe, your gun and there's one inside your ID."

Harvey didn't reply.

"There's also two on your bike, but I can see that's still at your home."

"What's your plan, Harvey?"

"The plan is coming," he replied. "For now, just keep following Larson."

"Ah, I can see the hard drive," said Reg, "it's video footage."

"How long is it?" asked Harvey.

"Looks to be about an hour's worth of two-minute clips. I think they roll the footage around, so it overwrites the earlier data with new data."

"Okay, can you watch the last thirty minutes? Let me know what's on there."

"I'm watching it now," said Reg. "It's like watching a really boring episode of that TV show about police chases."

12

DISCOVERY

Harvey sat in the back of the van with his back against Melody's seat. He answered a call, and held his phone to his ear. "Frank?"

"Stone, talk to me, I'm hearing strange things from above, being asked questions I don't know the answers-"

"Get me on the comms, Frank, my phone is compromised."

Harvey disconnected the call and turned the phone off. Melody turned in her seat.

"Compromised?" she asked.

"How else would they know where I am and where I live?"

"So we should assume all our phones are compromised?" asked Melody.

"Turn them on when you really need to, otherwise we use the comms."

"Reg, are the comms encrypted?"

"Yes they are. The phones are not though, it's a public network, so I don't control them. The boss is here, sit tight."

"Stone, I need an update. It's not looking good from my end," said Frank.

"I believe Stimson or Larson has managed to get my identity," said Harvey. "I found a body in my house last night, then the police came knocking, serious crime squad, and about thirty minutes ago, one of Stimson's guys tried to kill me. He took out a traffic cop, dumped him in the back of his patrol car and pulled us over just as we were tailing Larson."

"Do we have proof of that?"

"Of the body? Not yet."

"Of the kidnapping and the alleged assault of the police officer?"

"We have enough to keep the guy in custody. We cuffed him and left him on the side of the road, then called it in. I imagine he's getting a hiding in the back of a meat wagon as we speak."

"Where are you all now?"

"On the A12, sir," said Denver. "We're thirty minutes out from the city, maybe less."

"How would they of got to you?" asked Frank.

"It's not impossible that they have their own Reg," said Harvey.

"Whoa there," said Reg, "There's only one-"

"What about Mills and Cox?" said Frank.

"Larson saw us together in the manor house, sir," said Melody. "We have to assume we're known to them as well."

"Where's Larson now?" asked Frank.

"He's off the A12, heading into Stratford. He's being followed by Stimson's tough guy."

"His minder?" asked Frank.

"Yeah, we caught them having a breakfast meeting in the manor house, Larson, the goon and some woman."

"A woman?" asked Frank.

"Yes, sir, an unknown," said Melody.

"This is getting complex," said Frank. "Come back to base, we'll discuss."

"Negative, Frank, we're on the heels of Larson, and he's heading somewhere he doesn't want us to know about. We need to see what he's up to, and who he's with."

"Stone, you're aware that every policeman in East London is looking for you right now?"

"The story of my life, Frank."

"Harvey, tell me straight," began Frank. "Anything you want to tell us?"

"As it happens, Frank, yeah there is."

"Go on, I'm listening."

"I'd like to tell you I'm getting bored of having you poke your finger at me every time someone gets killed. We're on this guy, and for the first time, he doesn't know it. If I'm right and he's been watching our every move then this is the first time he won't know we're coming."

There was a silence while Frank thought.

"Okay, go," said Frank. "I'll be watching you all, and remember, we don't want any action, we're just observing."

"How come every time the boss tells Harvey and Melody to just observe, all hell breaks loose?" said Reg.

"Not this time, Tenant," said Frank. "I'm holding you accountable. If you see or hear anything that deviates from my orders, I want to know, and you'll be just as guilty as they are."

"Ah guys, look what you did," said Reg. Melody and Denver smiled at his remark.

"Sir?" said Melody.

"Go ahead."

"The manor house."

"What about it?" asked Frank.

Melody nodded for Harvey to explain.

"It's the perfect place to hold an auction of a priceless artefact. It's surrounded by miles of green, has no underground tunnels, and if they have airborne security, the chances of an airborne getaway are even slimmer," said Harvey.

"What are you saying?" asked Frank.

"I'm saying that the place is impossible to rob."

"Good, we might actually catch them then. If Larson is heading into town, he might be meeting the crew. It sounds like the breakfast was a recce, and he's pulling the team together now."

"Agreed, sir," said Melody.

"Okay, stay on them, report back and don't deviate."

"Copy that, sir," said Melody.

"Okay, Larson and the goon have both stopped at a warehouse in Stratford," said Reg. "There's nothing more conspicuous than a gloomy East London warehouse, right?"

"Send us the location, Reg," said Denver.

"You're looking at Tutbury Lane, it's off-"

"I know it, I know the warehouses too," said Denver. "You got a unit number?"

"Not yet, I'm zooming in, looks like it's the end unit of the first row, facing the main road."

"Any cars outside?" said Harvey.

"There's a few, looks like it's a busy place maybe a mechanic's garage. You can park on the road outside and see in through the fence. Don't drive in, it's a dead end, and probably full of yardies."

"Copy that, Reg," said Denver. "Thanks for the heads up."

"So what do you reckon about you having a bit of competition, Reg?"

"What do I reckon about what?"

"Competition, Reg. You know, whoever it is Larson has tracking our phones. Sounds like you might have some competition."

"Oh come on, any fool can track a phone," said Reg. "I mean if they were that good, *I'd* know about them."

"You sure about that?" asked Harvey. Harvey rarely got involved in the banter with Reg, but it was fun, and the team needed a lift in morale. "I mean, they must be pretty good to first of all, find out where I lived, hack my phone, and get my name."

"Child's play, Harvey, child's play."

"That gives me an idea," said Melody. "If we turned Harvey's phone on, could you see if it was being tracked and from *where* it was being tracked?"

"You're talking to the master, Melody."

"Okay, when this is done, and we're out of Stratford, you can have a go. We might find out where they're working from."

"Good call, nerd warfare," said Denver. "In the meantime, we're nearly there. Get yourselves set up. There's a shop over the road from the warehouses, we can park outside it and watch the play."

Denver reversed up onto the pavement and killed the engine. They had a perfect view across the road at the front of the warehouse. Melody set up her DLSR and zoom lens. Harvey used the scope. They both watched, but nothing happened.

"I don't see the BMW anywhere," said Melody.

"Inside maybe?" said Denver, who was keeping watch for passers-by, to make sure nobody looked in and saw the big camera and sighting scope. In East London, if someone saw a van parked up with surveillance taking place, the word would get around like wildfire that the police were closing in on something. A block of flats stood a few hundred yards away and would have been home to countless drug dealers, stolen goods, and probably hookers. It wasn't the nicest part of Stratford, and in those parts, people were street savvy.

"I'm going to take a closer look," said Harvey. He pulled his jacket on and slid the door open.

"Harvey, no. You heard Frank," said Melody.

"Harvey, don't do it," said Reg over the comms. "I'd have to get Frank, and he won't be happy."

"Give me five minutes," said Harvey. "If I'm not back, call it in, tell him I've been a bad boy."

"Oh Jesus, why is it every time we try and do something, we have to step off the line?" said Melody.

"Because staying on the line is not going to get us anywhere is it, Melody?" said Harvey. "Look across the road, the doors are shut. They're hardly likely to leave them open and let us watch them planning a robbery are they?"

"Even so, Harvey, we need more intel, and how we get intel is by being patient and planning. That's your mantra, right?"

"Yeah, that's right, Melody, it's what I live my life by."

"So why do you go off it all the time?"

"Because sitting here isn't going to give us a plan. Me going over there and taking a look will give us the intel we need to create a plan."

"Guys, guys, stop," said Denver. The shutter doors of the warehouse slid back a few metres, and the goon stepped out. Melody grabbed her camera and started to snap away. Harvey climbed back into the van and slid the door shut. The goon walked along the small lane outside the row of warehouses and checked the cars, then walked back to the shutter door and slid it open.

"He's checking the road's clear," said Melody. "Somebody's coming out."

The shutter door slid open further, and there in front of the team was a the rear end of a ten-year-old black taxi.

———

Sitting beside the taxi was the black BMW. The BMW's

reverse lights came on as soon as the shutter doors were fully open and the big saloon reversed out onto the concrete. The goon pulled the doors closed again. The screech of metal on metal carried across the road to the van.

"Did you see that?" asked Melody.

"Yeah, that's not good," said Denver.

"When that BMW pulls off, I'm going in," said Harvey.

"Harvey, what is it you expect to see in there?" said Melody.

"Answers." Harvey checked his Sig and slid it into his cargo pants. "I'll just have a look around, give us a head start."

"Remember, Harvey, you know I'll have to call this in don't you?" said Reg over the comms. "The big guy'll fry me if you go in."

"Are you a grass now, Reg?"

"Oh, please don't make me be the bad guy," whined Reg.

"The BMW is on the move," said Denver. He started the van and reversed it up behind the wall so it was completely out of sight.

"That's Larson. The goon is leaving too," said Reg. "How big is he? Is he as big as the last guy?"

"Bigger, I'd say, reminds me of Julios."

"And Julios was your teacher from killing school, right?" said Reg.

"Julios was my best friend, he taught me a lot of things."

"Yeah but he also taught you how to kill, didn't he?" said Reg. "My teachers just taught us maths and the gross domestic produce of some place I'll never go to."

"Reg, I get the impression you're lonely in there on your own," said Melody, breaking up the dead-end conversation.

"I'm not on my own, Melody, I've got Chief Inspector fun buckets sitting upstairs waiting for me to call him as soon as Harvey does something wrong."

"So you are a grass then?" said Harvey. "You know what they do to grasses in prison, Reg?"

"I'm guessing they don't get extra food?"

"You're right, but they do get a nice little cuddle in the evening," said Denver.

"That sounds nice," said Reg.

"You should try it," said Harvey. "I can even arrange it for you if you keep on going the way you are."

"Changing the subject, the BMW and the goon have left. They both turned left out of the warehouse compound. Are we going after them, or are we getting into trouble?" said Reg.

Harvey had slid the door open and had one foot out on the concrete.

"Harvey, get back in the van, we can come back," said Melody. "That's an order, let's go back to HQ, regroup and reassess. If you really want to get back here, we'll do it at night, on my terms, and I'll even come with you, but we need to brief Frank."

Harvey paused, and looked across at the garage. "I'll hold you to that, Melody Mills," said Harvey, sliding the side door of the van closed. "If Larson wants me out of the picture so much, he won't stop now. He couldn't get me arrested, and he couldn't kill me the first time, but who's to say he won't try again?"

13

SHOWED HANDS

REG HIT THE BUTTON SHORTCUT ON HIS KEYBOARD TO OPEN the shutters for the van to pull in. He closed it again and stood to pop the rear door open for Harvey.

"Hey, team. I missed you guys."

Harvey climbed out, stretched his arms upward, then folded to touch his toes. He clung to his feet for a few seconds, then slowly eased himself up, releasing a long breath. Reg looked on aghast.

"If I tried that, I'd get stuck and end up staring at my crotch for the rest of my life."

Harvey didn't reply.

Frank called down from the mezzanine, "Debrief, let's go."

The team didn't reply. Instead, they walked up to the meeting room and took up their usual positions. Reg sat on the couch, Denver sat on the arm of another couch, Melody stood by the coffee machine, waiting for it to finish filling the pot, and Harvey leaned on the wall by the door.

Frank stood by the whiteboard at the head of the room.

"Welcome back, team. Things are moving. What did we learn? The manor house?"

"Perfect for auctioning a priceless artefact," said Melody. "With the right security, there's little chance of it being robbed by a small team. The place is full of expensive art, Caravaggio, ancient pottery. You could use the frames of some of the painting's *alone* as a house deposit. Do we know how the buddha is being transported?"

"Not yet, there's no talk of it at all, it might already be in the country. Did you see the vault?"

"No, sir. We were preoccupied with Larson and his crew," said Melody.

"Okay, Larson. Tell me what you know."

"The photo's accurate, he hasn't changed his appearance. The phone we are tracking is correct, plus we bugged and chipped his car."

Frank turned to Reg. "Tenant, anything on the bug?"

"Not a bean, I pulled a WAV file from it and literally all we have is road noise. He hasn't uttered a word."

"Okay, who was he with?"

"Big guy, still an unknown, Stimson's minder."

"Another big man? Is he going to be a problem?" asked Frank to Harvey.

The team looked across to Harvey who rolled his eyes. "No, probably not."

Melody grinned.

"Are we tracking the big guy?" asked Frank.

"We have his phone," said Reg.

"Yeah, when they left the manor house they split into three cars," began Melody. "Larson took an Audi, the goon took the BMW, and the woman was picked up in a little red Porsche. The only one who isn't on LUCY is the woman."

We tailed Larson, but the goon was hanging back so we

couldn't get close. That was when we got pulled over, sir," said Denver.

"Okay, so stop there, before we go any further." Frank began to write on the board. "Manor house is perfect for an auction but almost impossible to rob. In my mind that makes it an ideal target for Stimson, he'll be all over that. You agree with that, Stone?"

Harvey didn't reply.

"Good. Larson isn't running the show, he's a puppet, a powerful puppet. Would you agree with *that* Stone?"

Harvey didn't reply.

"What if Larson *is* running the show?" said Melody. "How can we be sure that-"

"If Larson was there with Stimson's minder, I would imagine the minder is Stimson's eyes and ears. There's no way he's going to go to the manor house he's about to rob to have breakfast with the team he's getting to rob it." Frank paused. "Would you agree with that at least, Stone?"

"I agree with what you're saying, Frank, you don't need to ask. Trust me, when I don't agree you'll know about it."

"No ambiguity there then. Stone, if you were robbing a priceless buddha from the manor house, how would you go about it?"

"I thought about that. The vault is probably underground, there'll be a heavy security detail, but the buddha isn't there yet-"

"How you can so sure?"

"We could have walked out with any one of those paint-ings or pots with a toy knife. There was a poncy butler on the door, and no cameras. If I was Stimson, I'd take it in transit. Failing that, I'd wait until the place was empty of the public, which I'm sure it will be on auction day, and full of men that are collectively worth more than a small country. Men who have everything to lose and cash to pay for their lives."

"Hostages?"

"Yeah, hostages. I'd go in armed, hard and fast with enough men to cover the auction room while two or three more blow the vault. I'd stash the buddha inside the house, somewhere open to the public. If anyone gets caught, I'd make it look like the boys were stealing money from the rich buyers. The buddha would be hidden and not found on any person, and it can be picked up during a nice little breakfast with some friends a few weeks later when the whole thing has calmed down. If I was Stimson, I'd have found a few places behind wooden panelling or somewhere to stash the buddha."

"You thought hard about that?"

"Yeah, there's no possible way you'd get away with the buddha once the alarm has been raised, and there's no way the crew would get away either. They'd get a few years for armed robbery and would need paying off, but there's a load of guys out there that would risk that for their families, and Stimson isn't shy when it comes to spending money on something he wants. The crew will be lifers, men Stimson can trust, who know they will be looked after inside, and have their families looked after on the outside.

"No, he's not afraid to splash the cash." Frank gave Harvey's plan some thought. "What about Stimson? Surely he wouldn't be prepared to go away?"

"No he wouldn't, not with dedicated men like that, he'd have an exit, he may even go in as a buyer. A bystander as it were."

"Good analysis," said Frank. "Tenant, see what you can find on the security for the manor house, any locals firms, mobs or whatever."

Frank put Reg's name beside the manor house on the whiteboard.

"Moving on, so you were pulled over by traffic police? I want the full story. Mills, go."

"We were out of Braintree, heading for the A12, when the Volvo came from behind us. He gave two short blasts on the sirens and indicated for us to pull over-"

"First sign," said Harvey.

"Denver got out of the van, and the policeman told him to put his hands on the vehicle, without explanation, then he cuffed and searched Denver."

"Second sign," said Harvey.

"I got out and showed him my ID, and he shoved me up against the van and cuffed me."

"Third sign."

"That's when Harvey stepped out and gave himself up. He already knew Harvey's name and had him up against the van with the cuffs in his hand. That was when-"

"That was when I was sure he was fake," said Harvey.

"Why?"

"Two short blasts on the sirens on a quiet A-road? Not a traffic cop's style, they keep them off unless the roads are busy or it's high speed. The way he handled Denver, too rough, plus he gave no reason for the tug. He was rude and rough with Melody and cuffed her despite her ID and for no reason, then he knew my name."

"You're sure he knew your name?"

"Yeah, positive. Why would a white hat in the sticks know my name?"

"Because of the dead man in your bathtub?" asked Reg.

"No, we're talking deepest darkest sticks, not much chance of it being at the top of a traffic cop's priority list out there," said Harvey. "Lastly, the cop had three sets of cuffs on him. Pretty unlikely he carries *them* every day, right?"

"Right. So what did you do?" asked Frank.

"I told him what I thought."

"You told him what you thought?

"I put the guy down and cuffed him. Then unlocked these guys' handcuffs."

"That's when we found the real cop unconscious in the boot of the car, sir," said Melody.

"And what did you do with him?"

"Sat him on the ground leaning on the car," said Harvey. "I gave a call over his radio, took the dash cam and hard drive, and we got out of there."

"So nobody saw you?"

"Whoever drove past might have seen us, but no police saw us."

"What's with the questions, sir?" asked Melody.

"Well, Mills, every time you lot go out, I have to pull answers out of my backside for the mess you make."

"This wasn't us being cavalier, sir," said Melody.

"No, you're right. So I hear now your phones are compromised?"

"Only Harvey's for sure, but ours are off to be safe. We're relying on the comms until Reg can confirm the phones are safe to use."

"What's the plan to check that?"

"I'll go out, away from here. I'll turn my phone on, and Reg will be able to see if it's being tracked, and where the tracker is," said Harvey.

"Tenant, you can do that?" asked Frank.

"In my sleep, sir."

"So why isn't a basic security protocol like that in operation all the time? Is it something we can do constantly?"

"Okay, I'll get it set up," said Reg, slightly perplexed at his oversight.

"Has my phone been compromised?" asked Frank.

"I'll check," said Reg. "In the meantime, it's best to turn it off."

"Good. This is the type of thing we need to get better at, people. Now, talk to me about the warehouse."

"Stratford, sir. Old warehouse, rough part of town," said Denver.

"We followed Larson and the goon there," said Melody, "They weren't there long and then they left again."

"But?" said Frank. "I can sense a but coming."

"We got a glimpse inside, sir."

"Tell me what you saw."

"A black taxi, sir. Reg has checked the plates, it was Arthur Bell's taxi."

"What else did you see?"

"Nothing, sir, the door was only open for a moment while Larson pulled his car out."

"He either picked something up or dropped something off, Frank," said Harvey. "I'm going back tonight."

"Are you? I thought it was me that gave the orders, Stone."

"Not when it comes to people trying to kill me, Frank. With all due respect." Harvey spoke the last words slowly and clearly.

Frank stared at Harvey for a second. "Okay, let's make it worthwhile. Mills, you're going in with him. Cox, Tenant, you'll both be outside. What's security like?"

"There's a guy on the gate, easily avoided, he's more likely there to stop pikeys getting in," said Harvey. "There's a single door on the warehouse with a pull-down shutter over it and a large sliding door."

"Plan?"

"I'll get into the single door. The large door screeches and will wake up most of London."

"Alarm?"

"Doubt it, Frank. There's a stolen taxi inside that

belonged to the dead guy the police found in my house. If I had that taxi, I wouldn't be setting an alarm."

"Anyone inside? Security detail?"

"Only one way to find out."

"Okay get in, have look around, bug it and get out." Frank turned to address the whole room. "Anything else I need to know?"

"Actually, sir, yes," began Reg. "The dash cam Harvey ripped out of the police car had some pretty quite surprising footage on it."

14

BREAK IN

It was four am when Harvey sheared the locks on the shutter door. Harvey quietly put the car jack he'd used to one side, and pulled the shutter up, revealing a single door with a glazed upper panel. The wood was soft, cheap and old, and gave easily when Harvey slipped his jimmy bar in and leaned a little weight on it. The lock remained in position, but the entire door was forced away from the frame and opened easily.

Harvey stood in the doorway listening.

"What are you waiting for?" Melody whispered.

Harvey tapped his watch and held up one index finger. Melody noted his frown and look of concentration. She stepped back and checked behind her; the compound of warehouses and garages was clear of people. The security hut a hundred yards away was lit softly from inside, allowing the guard to read his book.

Melody checked across the street and saw the van parked outside the shop. She couldn't see any movement or lights from inside, the tinted windows hid Denver and Reg well. Even Reg's screens didn't light the interior of the van.

She sensed movement in the corner of her eye, Harvey was moving in. She stepped slowly behind him, watching for an attack to come from the shadows. The warehouse smelled like a mechanic's garage; the air was thick with the smell of motor oil and dust.

Melody had her Sig drawn and held it in two hands aiming beyond Harvey into the darkness. Harvey stepped out the little hallway into the large warehouse space and disappeared into the gloom. Melody stood in the doorway listening for his footsteps but heard nothing. She lowered her night vision goggles and saw Harvey standing to her left beside the taxi. Harvey didn't wear NV. He allowed his senses to adjust to the darkness. When he was happy that they were alone, he motioned to Melody to turn the lights on. She found the switches on the wall beside her. Even in the green NV she could see the grime on the switch.

She closed her eyes before flicking the switch and lifted the goggles before opening them again. The warehouse looked like a far different place than it had with the goggles on.

"Stay near the door, in case security see the light."

Melody stayed put, but planted three audio bugs in various places nearby while she waited; one on top of a large space heater, one below a workbench beneath the light switch, and one on a rack of metal shelving behind her. She leaned against a wooden crate and watched Harvey move around the taxi. The space around the parked car was empty, save for a few hessian sacks that were sat on the dirty floor. An old tool chest stood open, and an array of tools had been thrown inside it. It was a far cry from Denver's set up and his meticulously clean working environment. A stack of wheels stood in the corner beside the shutter door and a large hydraulic car jack sat beside them. In front of the taxi was a pile of car seats, semi-covered in thick blue plastic sheets, and behind that was an old, battered forklift truck.

Harvey placed a bug inside the black cab. "Rear seats have gone," he said, just loudly enough for her to hear.

"They're there in front." She nodded with her head when he looked at her. "They're stripping it down to hide the murder?"

Harvey glanced at the pile of seats and stared back at the taxi. He stepped over closer but didn't move anything. Harvey glanced back at Melody.

Melody looked at the crate she leaned on. It was a heavy wooden box fixed to a wooden pallet. She stood away from it to read the sides, but the language was foreign. Whatever it said, it was written in German.

"Harvey?"

Harvey saw Melody looking at the box and joined her.

"German," she said.

"Car parts?" said Harvey.

"You know what's made in Germany?"

Harvey stepped back to the tool chest and found a large flathead screwdriver. He rejoined Melody, who was taking photos of the writing.

She hit the button on her ear-piece that opened comms, "Reg."

"Go ahead," came Reg's reply.

"Sending you a photo, need it translated quick smart."

She hit send on her phone, then turned it off quickly. She watched as Harvey worked his way carefully around the top of the box, easing the lid up without leaving marks in the soft wood. He prised one end up enough to slip his fingers underneath, and yanked the lid upwards, then carefully lowered it to the floor.

"Direct translation is a bit confusing, Melody, but it basically says, *Highly Volatile*."

Harvey was carefully lifting a plastic sheet that covered the contents of the box. Melody held out her hand to stop him.

"Did you hear Reg?" she asked.

Harvey didn't reply. The frown deepened on his face. He lifted the plastic fully and stared down at the mass of plastic explosives. He raised his eyes to Melody.

"That's a lot of explosives," said Melody.

Harvey pulled the lid back on and hammered it closed with his fist.

"Let's go," he said. "Denver, extract." They stepped outside and heard the warble of the van's exhaust from across the street.

"Go, I'll catch you up," said Harvey, as he turned to pull the shutter door down.

Melody turned and ran to the wall she and Harvey had climbed over. She checked behind her to make sure the coast was clear, then pulled herself up and waited for Harvey to join her.

Harvey sprinted from the shadows and leapt up. He caught hold of the top of the wall and was down the other side in matter seconds. Melody took a final glance back towards the warehouse, but as she did, headlights appeared at the entrance to the compound. She laid low on the top of the wall. More headlights appeared after the first, another car. Melody lowered herself down and stood beside Harvey as Denver pulled the van up on the street.

The sliding door slid open, and they climbed in. "Go, go, go." Denver pulled away as the door pulled shut, and the team sat in silence for a while until they were clear of the area.

Melody was the first to speak.

"We're too late," she said. "The explosives are already here, and it looked like two cars just arrived as we left."

"How much?" asked Denver.

"PX5? Enough to blow a hole in London big enough to fit another city in. About a hundred kilos."

Denver's eyes widened. "A hundred kilos of plastic explosives?"

"Sitting on a pallet in a warehouse in the arse-end of London," said Melody.

"Not for long," said Harvey. "That's what the cabs are for."

"What?" said Melody.

"It's obvious. They didn't strip the cab down to hide the murder, they stripped it down to fit the explosives inside." Harvey took a breath. "That cab's going to be driven through London and detonated somewhere busy."

"Stimson?"

"Sadly, yes."

"Why would Stimson do that? He's a diamond thief, not a terrorist," said Melody.

"I know, it doesn't make sense."

"Reg, can you get us a list of all known auction houses in the city of London? Not West London, in the city," said Harvey.

"Easy," replied Reg.

"Then tell me which ones have a day scheduled as closed in the next few days, should be on their website."

"What are you saying, Harvey?" said Melody.

"I'm saying the auction isn't happening in Wethersfield, that's a decoy. Stimson planted that intel to lead us away from the real auction."

"Frank got us that information," said Melody.

"Where from? His phone?" said Harvey. "We've already seen my phone is compromised." Harvey let that information settle in, then said, "The robbery will take place at the same time as that taxi drives into London and detonates. They'll be so much chaos that getting away with a tiny little statue will be easy."

"There are a number of auction houses in the City of London itself, but notably, there's one on Queen Victoria Street, which happens to be directly behind St Paul's Cathedral. It's closed in three days time for a private event, according to the website's calendar."

"Queen Victoria Street? That's where we found Hague, he was on foot heading towards St Paul's," said Harvey.

"You think the buddha has been there all along?" said Melody.

"It makes sense," said Harvey. "Imagine it, they tried to do the heist with Hague as the decoy, but we nailed him, foiled their plan, so they aborted the heist. They found out who we were from the bloody videos people took on the bridge and set up a decoy auction out in the sticks. Meanwhile, their tech guy hacked my identity, they planted a body to get me arrested, then tried to take me out in Essex." He paused. "And now this. They know we're getting closer."

The team sat silently and thought on Harvey's synopsis.

"Denver," said Harvey, "let's go see this auction house."

"Copy that," replied Denver.

"Even Stimson wouldn't stoop so low, would he?"

"That depends doesn't it," said Harvey.

"On?"

"His motive."

"His motive?"

"Yeah, what's driving him to pull such a crazy stunt."

"The priceless buddha?"

"The Stimsons are responsible for the biggest heists in recent history. They've been doing this for as long as I can remember," said Harvey. "And you know what?"

"What?"

"They've never killed a single person in any of their heists."

"Not a single one?"

"Nothing more than the butt of a rifle in a security guard's face. So why would they change that habit now, and potentially kill hundreds of people?"

"His motivation's changed," said Melody.

"It looks like it, but there's more."

"More?"

"Think about what you just saw, Melody."

She turned to face him in her seat, "The taxi?"

"And?"

"The wheels?"

Harvey didn't reply.

"The seats?"

Harvey raised his eyebrow.

"There was a pile of seats," she said, then her eyes widened. "Too many for one taxi." Cogs fell into place. She gasped. "There's more than one taxi."

15

FALLEN HERO

"How far, Denver?" asked Melody.

"We're coming up to Liverpool Street, less than three minutes away," Denver replied.

"What's the plan?" asked Melody.

"I just want to take a look, see the auction house, see what Stimson is likely to do," said Harvey.

"Looking at the satellite imagery," said Reg, "from the auction house, they'd have a clear run down to the river, if they had-"

"A boat waiting," finished Melody. "They'd be away in no time at all, they could have a car waiting at literally any point along the river."

"I was going to say that, you always steal my thunder, Melody," said Reg. "I'll call Frank, and tell him what we're doing, he should be in HQ by now."

Reg dialled Frank's number and waited for him to answer.

"Wait," said Harvey. "Your phone is on?"

"Well yeah, it works better when its-"

"Turn it off!" shouted Melody.

"Tenant?" Frank answered the call. "What's the update?"

Just then a car slammed into the side of the van, forcing it into oncoming traffic. Denver's head crashed into the door and shattered the glass. Reg was thrown back off his seat and onto Harvey who was sat on the floor behind Melody.

Denver pulled the van back to the correct side of the road, but the car held its nose into the side of the van. The two vehicles were locked, neither one dropping their throttles. Smoke rose from the screeching tyres and the smell of burning rubber filled the air.

"It's a taxi," called Denver.

Harvey jumped up and slid the side door of the van open, but it was jammed by the damage and the front wing of the taxi. He pulled his Sig and fired two rounds through the small gap into the taxi's wheel. The taxi slowed a little, allowing Harvey to shove the door open, but the door's rails were smashed, and it fell off onto the road. The taxi bounced over it, accelerated again and slammed once more into the side of the van, nudging it further and further sideways.

Harvey put his Sig into his waistband, and leapt from the van onto the taxi's bonnet. He grabbed hold of the windscreen wipers. They twisted and bent under his weight, but he held on, his legs swinging across the front of the car's rounded bonnet.

The sound of the two battling engines was all Harvey could hear, and the road was filled with smoke. People ran from the sliding wreckage. The van drove on with the taxi wedged into its side, both engines fighting for control.

Harvey let go with one hand and pulled his Sig once more, but the driver yanked the steering wheel just as he aimed, and Harvey's legs swung across to the passenger side. His feet scraped the road just inches from the tyre. Denver saw Harvey's struggle and turned hard into the front of the taxi, pushing it off the road to stop Harvey from being crushed. The driver held the wheel firm. As the taxi careered into the roadside barrier, Harvey was dragged off the car.

The team watched in horror as Harvey's body disappeared from view and the taxi bounced; its rear wheels drove effortlessly across Harvey's leg. Melody turned sharply in her seat to see Harvey roll into the middle of the road. The taxi came to a stop. Denver was out the van like a shot. He forced his driver's door open as Melody opened hers. She ran back to Harvey, frantically trying to raise Frank on the comms, while Denver yanked the taxi's driver door open.

The Middle-Eastern driver had smashed his face on the steering wheel when Denver had forced him off the road. He raised his bloodied face and looked ahead of him, confused. He turned and looked up at Denver as Denver's fist connected with his jaw. Denver stood upright, held onto the open door with one hand and the roof of the taxi with the other, then brought his foot down hard on the man's face again and again.

Sirens sounded in the distance, and the taxi driver roused himself at the sound. He raised his arm to stop Denver's attack and looked behind him. Then he smiled cruelly at Denver. Denver saw the man's left hand reaching across to the passenger floor. A tangled mass of wires was connected to a home-made switch. He glanced into the back of the taxi and saw that there were no seats.

Denver threw himself into the driver's seat on top of the man and wrestled his arm from the wires, but the man was strong and held on. His fingers were slowly working towards the switch while Denver tried to pull him away.

With no other choice, Denver stamped on the gas pedal. His right leg dragged along the ground as he steered the taxi away from the van and the team. The Middle-Eastern man struggled harder, but Denver pulled his foot in and pushed back on the driver, pinning him to the seat. He held the driver's wrist and tried to pry the wires from his bony hand but the man held fast. With his right hand, Denver steered the accelerating taxi away from other traffic. The wing mirror smashed off as he passed too close to another car and the driver got out and began to shout.

Denver rounded a long, sweeping bend and came to a straight. He held the steering wheel with his leg, and began punching the driver's head furiously. The man was shouting in a foreign language, repeating the same sentence over and over.

Grabbing the wheel once more, Denver slid the taxi around a corner too fast. It bounced off the curb, but maintained its speed. He rounded the long chicane of Queen Victoria Street where the road merged with the embankment, and, seeing no other choice, aimed the speeding taxi towards the river.

The high curb tore the front wheel off the chassis and the car's rear end bounced hard, launching into the air. Denver braced for the impact. The crazed driver seized the opportunity he'd been waiting for and lunged for the switch as the car crashed into the water.

The river muffled the explosion, but the blast rocked Blackfriar's Bridge, shook the surrounding trees and smashed the glass of cars passing by. A rush of water surged high into the air.

Within moments, the river had returned to its steady flow of brown water. The only sign of the taxi was the thousands of bubbles that surfaced then dissipated, disappearing as quickly as the taxi had been destroyed.

16

BEAST'S REVENGE

HARVEY LAUNCHED HIMSELF FROM THE SIDE DOOR ONTO the front of the taxi that was wedged into the side of the van. Both vehicles were powering through the crash, each driver battling to bring the other to a stop. Harvey clung to the wiper with one hand and with the other reached behind him and pulled his weapon from his waist. He brought it up to fire, but the driver pulled hard on the steering wheel, sending Harvey to the far side of the car's bonnet. His leg fell off the smooth surface, and his foot dragged perilously close the wheels scraping the floor. His felt the burn of the rubber through his thick boots.

The taxi ploughed on with one blown tyre. The driver straightened up, and Harvey clung on for his life, desperately trying to keep his leg from being dragged under the wheel.

Denver saw his chance and steered the van into the taxi's path, trying to stop the cab from crushing Harvey into the railings, but it was too late. Harvey was dragged from the car, and his hand ripped off the sharp metal wiper arm. The rear wheels bounced across his thigh, and Harvey rolled to a stop face down on the tarmac.

His leg pounded and his hands were wet with warm sticky blood, but all he could do was close his eyes and rest his head on the hard road.

It felt like an eternity, sleep washed over him, deep and welcoming. He was no longer laying on the road but was warm in fresh, clean sheets. All around him were featureless white walls and air so clean he could taste the sea. He imagined a long, empty beach with the sea far off to his right. Long wild grass grew in clumps to his left, beyond was a blur of pastel yellow and green. He ran on the sand. He ran so fast he thought he would trip and stumble, but she held out her hand. It was Hannah, enticing him to catch her, faster, faster, her long legs bounded easily over the sand. Her bare feet barely left a mark.

He was closer now, the sun was stronger, the light was brighter. He squinted but ran harder. Tears streamed from his eyes. He reached out, step after step, bound after bound in the soft sand, then, at last, he felt her hand slip through his fingers. Harder, faster, he pushed, his breathing in time with his effort, blinded by the bright light he ran on and on. He could hear her laughing. "Run, Harvey, you can catch me."

He growled loudly and pushed harder than ever. His little arms pumped wildly and his legs were numb, but all the power in his child's body surged through them. Reaching out once more, he felt her fingers, long and slender. He held his hand there, groping in his blindness as he pumped his other arm and legs. He growled again, long and hard and pushed with everything he had.

His hand found hers, and gripped it tight, like a man's grip. She laughed in the light then stumbled and they fell together and rolled. He came to a stop on his back, and she laid across him, panting. "You did it, Harvey, you caught me." He was no longer a boy, he was a man. But his sister retained her youth, her perfect skin and welcoming smile. Kindness shone from her eyes and the wind ruffled her long, blonde hair.

"You did it, Harvey." She smiled up at him.

———————

A cold wind rushed over Harvey. His body shook and his muscles convulsed. He tried to curl up but his leg wouldn't move, and a dull ache set into his back. Something wailed in the distance. The sound grew closer. The bright, white walls and the clean air turned to grey. He licked his parched lips and tasted grit and blood.

He opened his eyes.

"Harvey?" A silhouette kneeled over him. "Harvey, talk to me." He closed his eyes again.

Harvey clenched his fist and felt the stab of pain across his palm, but clenched tighter and harder, squeezing the blood from his grip.

"Don't move, Harvey, stay there, it's okay, there's help coming."

The realisation that he was laying on a road struck him, and he rolled painfully onto his back.

"Don't move, Harvey. Can you talk? Can you hear me?"

He opened his eyes one more and saw nothing but the dome of St Paul's Cathedral, black against the grey sky.

"Here, take some water." The woman held a bottle to his mouth and poured him a sip. He wanted more and reached for it, but she held him down. "Stay there, Harvey." He swallowed and felt the water release the tension in his throat.

"The taxi?"

"It's gone," said the woman. "You nearly killed yourself."

Recognition came to him, and he stared at her. Her long hair rested on his neck as she leaned over him. "I know that smell."

"Harvey, you've had a serious accident, stay down, just relax."

"I know you," he rasped.

"Of course you do." She put her hand on his face and wiped moisture from his eye with her thumb. "It's me, Melody."

"Melody," he said. The wailing grew louder. More people stood around him. Melody spoke loudly to them. "Move away, give him space." Harvey saw them holding their phones. A man in a bright yellow jacket helped her move people away, and the ambulance parked alongside him. Two men in bright green knelt by his side.

"Mr Stone, can you hear me?" said the first man.

Harvey didn't reply.

The man stared into Harvey's eyes. "Can you hear me? Can you tell me where it hurts?" The man was feeling along Harvey's legs for broken bones.

"Come closer," said Harvey.

The man leaned into him so Harvey could talk into his ear.

"Get me up."

"Oh no, you're going on a stretcher my friend, you won't-"

"Get me up, now," said Harvey. He turned his head to find Melody, his eyes wild. "Get me up, Melody."

"Harvey, no. Let them do their jobs."

"What's your name?" said Harvey to the second EMT, the older of the men who was filling out a report on a tablet. He looked down at Harvey.

"My name's Jim, Mr Stone."

"Jim, tell your friend to stop checking for broken bones and help me up."

"You're clearly a brave man, Mr Stone, but as my colleague-"

"I'll do you both a deal." The two men listened. "If you

help me up and I begin to fall, you can stop me falling and put me the ambulance. But if I don't fall, and can stand, I walk away with my friend here."

"Sir, unfortunately-"

"Am I a grown man?"

"Yes, Mr Stone."

"So let me make a grown man's decision. If you don't help me up, I'll damn well get up myself, and that'll be the end of it."

"Harvey, you can't-"

"I can do what I like, Melody," he said calmly but sharply. "Are you going to help me up?"

The older of the two nodded at the first one, and they knelt either side of Harvey. Harvey bent his good leg and felt them pull his shoulders up. He pushed against them and felt the blood rush to his head, dizzying him.

"Easy now, come on, sit in the ambulance." The two men each held an arm.

"Okay," said Harvey. "Let me go."

Melody stood in front of him shaking her head. Harvey put the weight on his bad leg and breathed out, letting the pain in, controlling it, dominating it, as it scoured his leg for new places to hurt. He put more weight on and the pain increased. Still he stood, defiant.

"Thank you, both," said Harvey.

Melody stepped across the road and stood beside Harvey as the two EMTs moved away. She put her arm around him, and he rested his arm on her shoulders. He limped across to the van where Reg stood.

The look on Reg's face was sour. Tears rolled freely from his eyes.

"Reg, where's Denver?" asked Melody.

Reg didn't reply. He just stood and stared, shaking his head. He stood paralysed, looking dumbfounded between

Harvey and Melody. They stepped in closer. Harvey put his other arm up to Reg's shoulder, and Melody did the same. The three of them stood like that for several minutes, holding each other. The emotion ran through the group. At first, Harvey felt he was holding his two colleagues in a time of tragedy, then he felt the anger and loss wash over him, and felt as if it was them that held and comforted him.

Policemen broke up the huddle and took them to one side of the street. Melody discreetly showed him her badge and asked him to wait for Frank Carver to arrive. She and Reg slumped to the ground, but Harvey stood leaning against the wall. He put more weight on his bad leg for longer periods each time. Melody rested her head against his good leg and closed her eyes.

Harvey knew the power of adrenalin, he knew it would render the team powerless once its magical effects wore off. He kept himself charged and ran through the events in his head. Everything had changed. It was all different now. He looked up at St Paul's Cathedral across the street and wondered what might have been.

The team's sleek Audi drew up beside them. The driver side door opened and Frank stepped out the car. He pulled his long jacket around him and tied the belt, then folded his collar up against the wind. It was only then that Harvey realised the wind was strong and cold. His leather jacket had saved his skin and bore the brunt of the fierce British winter breeze.

Frank stood before them.

Melody looked up at him, but didn't stand. "I'm sorry, sir."

"You've nothing to be sorry for," said Frank with strength in his voice. It was just the four of them on the pavement opposite the cathedral. Frank waited for a full minute before speaking.

17

LURING THE MONSTER

"WE JUST LOST A GOOD MAN, THE WORLD JUST LOST A GOOD man, and Denver's family just lost everything," said Frank. "We need to act now, grieve later. I know it's hard, and if you want out. Now's the time to leave."

They were all silent.

"Let's recap what we've got," said Frank.

"We believe that the auction isn't going to take place in the manor house, that was a diversion from Stimson," said Harvey.

"Okay," said Frank. He was engaged and listening.

"We believe the auction will take place at an auction house on Queen Victoria Street, that's a hundred yards from where we're standing."

Harvey saw the cogs turning in Frank's head.

"We also believe that the buddha is already there in the vault."

"So the explosion was meant to be a distraction for the robbery?" Asked Frank.

"Yeah, we found Arthur Bell's taxi inside the warehouse, the seats had been stripped out ready for the explosives."

"And?"

"Plus the seats of at least two more taxis."

"And?"

"About a hundred kilos of plastic explosives."

"There's two more taxis rigged to blow?" asked Frank.

"We believe so, sir."

"This is Stimson we're talking about, loud explosions are not his style."

"Harvey thinks his motivation has changed," said Melody.

Frank nodded. "I'd agree with that, the entire strategy has changed, but he's been through a lot of trouble to get us out of the way. The manor, the cop. Are the phones still compromised?"

"We believe so, sir. They knew exactly where we were," said Reg.

"And probably where we are now," said Harvey.

"Exactly," said Frank. "So we need to move fast before they strike again. The taxis were stolen, they're hard to spot, easier to transport explosives. No-one would look twice at a taxi driving through here."

"But *we* needed to be diverted," said Melody.

"Yes, but not killed. Stimson isn't a killer remember," said Frank.

"So why were we attacked and nearly blown up?" asked Reg.

"The motivation got stronger," said Harvey. He pushed himself from the wall and winced as he limped to stand closer to the others. Melody put her hand on his arm, but he nodded to reassure her that he was okay standing on his own. "Whatever pressure is on Stimson to get that buddha, it recently got a lot stronger. Whatever is driving him to do the heist has recently become more pressing." Harvey thought on his own words. "Time is running out."

"Time is running out? asked Melody.

"Reg can you tell us if the auction house is closed now?" asked Harvey.

"Sure, I'll fire up the computers and see if I can-"

"Or you could walk around the corner and see if there's anything outside, like a timetable. Public auctions often have a notice behind glass like a courtroom," said Harvey.

"Oh, okay, that's easier," said Reg.

"Keep your comms open," said Frank as Reg walked away and disappeared around the corner.

"So, I'm guessing you'll be starting at the top, and finding out why Stimson's motivation has stepped up?" asked Frank.

"Seems like a good place to start," said Harvey.

"And how exactly do you plan on doing that? Time *is* running out, after all."

"There's three players here, not including Stimson, because he never leaves the house it seems."

"Right."

"Larson, clever bastard, one step ahead the entire time."

"Agreed."

"The goon, who doesn't really pose much of an issue until we come to take Stimson out, which isn't top priority here is it. Our priority is stopping the bombs going off so the auction can run, and the buddha can be removed from the vault safely and taken away someplace else."

"I'd agree with that loosely. Who's the third player?"

"Al Sayan."

"I told you not to go there, Stone."

"You want me to finish this, you need to trust me. Al Sayan is the key. Do you honestly believe that Stimson is responsible for what just happened to Denver?"

Frank looked at Harvey, sighed, then nodded slowly. "That changes everything," he said.

"While we waste time chasing Stimson and Larson, Al Sayan is picking us off, making it easier for them," said

Harvey. "We need to turn our attention here to the one who's calling shots."

The team were silent.

"First job," said Harvey. "We need to lure them out. Go somewhere easy to find, somewhere we can't run away. Once we see who comes after us, we'll see who's calling the shots here."

"That's a terrible plan, it doesn't make sense," said Melody.

Harvey smiled. "Did you see the taxi driver?"

"Yeah."

"British?"

"Middle Eastern at a guess."

"Right," said Harvey. "We'll get out of here, go somewhere with an open space and less people, somewhere a bomb could go off and not hurt anyone but us."

"You've lost the plot."

"They're tracking us, we're being hunted. Don't you see it?" said Harvey. "Let's not take the mountain to Mohammed, let him come to us."

"You have a plan I presume?" said Frank.

"I take the phones, stand in the middle of a field or a car park or something. Then two things will happen."

Melody was intrigued, but concerned.

"Reg will see the phone's interception."

"And?"

"Someone will turn up, possibly in the second black cab."

"And what good will that do?

"Two things, if the driver is British, which I doubt he is, Stimson's running the show, and we prod the driver for information. My speciality."

"And if he's-"

"If he's Middle Eastern, he won't talk, but he won't need to."

"Why not?

"Because if he's one of Al Sayan's men, it means that it is Al Sayan increasing the pressure on Stimson. We have a direction."

"You're putting yourself in the line of fire, Stone."

"Denver just drove a taxi rigged with explosives into the Thames so we could live. Let's make it count. You have a Diemaco in the van?" Harvey asked Melody.

"Sure," said Melody.

"You can take him out."

There was a long pause. Melody and Frank both knew the plan would give them direction. It was a loose plan, but it was all they had.

"What happens if the phones aren't intercepted?" asked Melody.

"Plan B."

"What's plan B?"

"Make a new plan," said Harvey. The comment wasn't meant to be funny, it was a statement that perfectly summed up their predicament. They had only one option.

"How are you feeling, Stone? Are you sure you're up to this?" asked Frank.

Harvey stared at him.

"Well, just let me know if you need anything, you look like crap, are you guys-"

"We'll be fine, sir," said Melody. "Are you going to see-"

"Denver's family? Yes."

"Please pass on the condolences of the team, sir. We all loved him. I can't believe he's gone," said Melody.

"I'm supposed to go down to the river now. There's more questions to be answered I'm sure," said Frank.

"What's to say?" said Harvey. "Denver's a hero. If it wasn't for him that four-hundred-year-old cathedral standing there would be levelled, and none of us would be stood here talking."

"He's a hero alright, but that doesn't make the news any easier to break to his family."

"He was close to his mum," said Melody. "Would you like me to go? You know, it's sometimes better coming from a woman."

"That's kind of you, Mills. But there's some things that need to come from me. You three have enough on your plate."

Reg returned from around the corner and walked towards the rest of the team. Frank turned to him and watched the small-framed man scurry along in the cold.

"There'll be a service?" asked Melody.

"Of that I'm sure," replied Frank glancing back. Then he turned to face St Paul's Cathedral. "We'll all be there."

Reg returned to the group. "Closed, no sign of anything, security in reception."

"Good, we still have time," said Harvey. "Let's do this."

"Did I ever tell you all about my wife?" asked Frank as the team made ready to go.

"No, sir," said Melody.

"She was a lovely woman really, caring and the rest. Did the things for me most men wouldn't do for themselves. Looked after me. We had a good many years together too. We travelled, we ate well, saw things some people only ever seen in photos. Jan was a good woman, the best. Salt of the earth. You know what I'm saying?"

The team nodded slowly.

"I lost her, three years ago. Some bastard felt that the time was right to destroy the lives of those around him." Frank stared at them with watery eyes. "You remember the Bow Street bomb?"

Melody's eyes widened. "She was on that?"

"Same carriage. She didn't stand a chance."

"That was Al Sayan too. What exactly are you saying, sir?" asked Melody.

"What am I saying? I don't know really." He huffed. "Loss? Hate?" He sighed. "Someone I respect a great deal once told me something that I'll never forget." Frank looked up at the sky and searched for the words. "Sometimes a man does something so bad, so evil, that society has an obligation to seek revenge, to right the wrong. And sometimes, those who have been so badly wronged are owed so much that they earn the opportunity to enact that revenge. For it's those that suffer the most who most deserve the closure that retribution brings." Frank turned to Harvey. A tear ran freely from Frank's eye.

Harvey gave an indiscernible nod.

"What am I saying?" said Frank, turning to Melody and Reg. "Go get them. For Denver."

———

They stripped the van of everything they needed and loaded it all into the Audi Frank had left for them. Reg removed his laptop, a mobile antenna and the mobile comms receiver.

Harvey helped Melody remove her Peli cases, surveillance equipment, two Heckler and Koch MP5s and her favourite, the Diemaco. It was a 7.62mm calibre assault rifle with a telescopic scope. The rails on the underside could hold either a red-dot laser or a grenade launcher. It was an awesome looking weapon and Melody's choice of weaponry for long range. The rifle also had a selector that changed the action from single shot to three-round bursts or full auto. Melody preferred the accuracy of single shot, but would quickly shift to three-round bursts if her position was compromised.

Frank spoke to the officer in charge at the scene and

arranged for the van to be taken to headquarters. He then tossed Harvey the keys to the Audi. "I'd wish you luck, but..." He paused, unable to find the words. He knew he was sending his remaining team off into the unknown, short-handed and emotionally scarred, but there was little he could do in such a short amount of time.

"For Denver, sir," said Melody.

"For Denver," replied Frank. He turned and took the longest walk of his life down to the river, where divers and investigators tried to piece the puzzle together, and scared onlookers filmed the scenes on their mobile phones.

Harvey tossed the keys to Melody.

"Why am I driving?" she asked.

"It's got four wheels," replied Harvey.

Reg had begun to set himself up in the back. He placed the small antenna on the roof and ran the cable down beside the rubber door trim. His laptop sat on the seat beside him and he placed the comms unit on the parcel shelf with the headphones plugged in and hanging on the headrest.

Melody's equipment was loaded into the boot and several pairs of binoculars and her scope were unboxed and kept loose beside Reg.

"Okay, before we move, let's do a comms check," said Reg.

"Stone," said Harvey pushing the button on his ear-piece once.

"Copy."

"Mills," said Melody.

"Loud and clear," confirmed Reg. "Comms is good. My connection to the satellite will be slow without the powered v-Sat unit the van had, but I'll see what I can do with the modems I have, and create an SSL VPN back to headquarters. This laptop won't run LUCY so well, so I'll be using the power of the command centre and just viewing the visual over the link to keep the bandwidth down, it should mask our IP as well."

"Sounds technical, Reg," said Harvey. He slid the action back on his Sig and chambered a round, flicked the safety on, and put the weapon back in his waist. "Yep, that works."

Melody climbed into the driver seat and pulled the door closed. She started the engine and pulled her seat belt across her chest. "Where are we going to do this?" she asked.

"Somewhere with little to no people, but close enough that we can get back here, quickly," said Harvey. "Reg, tell me what you see on satellite."

"How big does the space need to be?"

"Big enough for a car to explode with no collateral damage."

"Okay, the nearest large empty space I can see is Wanstead Flats. There'll be a dog walkers, maybe even some dogging action, but we can probably park out of the way."

"Which way?" asked Melody.

"A13, A406," said Harvey. "We'll be against the traffic this time of day."

Harvey slid his belt across when Melody put her foot down. The Audi's powerful engine kicked in, and before he knew it, they were leaving the city.

"Where's your phones?" asked Harvey.

Melody pulled her phone from her pocket, and Reg passed his forward over Harvey's shoulder.

"Here goes, Reg are you ready?"

"I'm activating the scanner now, it'll effectively use LUCY's tracking mechanism, and provide a bandwidth monitor. If somebody else starts tracking the same phone, my tracking bandwidth will be affected, then I can start identifying the source."

"In English, Reg?"

"It's like water running through a pipe. If you turn one tap on, you'll get full flow, but if a second tap is turned on, the flow of the first tap will decrease."

"Okay, sounds easy enough," said Harvey, glancing across to Melody with his eyebrows raised. "Turning on the first phone now."

Harvey turned Reg's on first, then five minutes later turned Melody's on, and then another five minutes later, he turned his own on.

"The last phone is on, Reg. You got them on screen?"

"Yep, all clear," replied Reg. "I have three flashing operatives and three bandwidth monitors running. I've set audio alerts up to sound when the bandwidth drops below a certain threshold."

"Right, next can you look for missing persons?"

"Missing persons?" asked Melody.

"Missing persons," confirmed Harvey. "We've still got two taxi drivers missing. It'll be useful to see if we can get the number plates, so we don't stumble upon some poor old cabbie eating his sandwiches."

"You think they'd keep the plates on? I would have thought they'd swap them out," said Reg.

"Might do, might not. No harm in knowing, is there?" replied Harvey.

They pulled into a parking area in the wide, open space of Wanstead Flats within less than thirty minutes. The car park sat on the edge of a large triangle of grass, which was bordered on all three sides by roads. There was a lake near one corner and a few clumps of various trees spread sporadically across the expanse of grass.

"No taxis in sight," said Reg.

Then the laptop omitted a soft beep.

"Bingo," said Reg. "It's Harvey's phone."

Beep.

"There's yours, Melody, bandwidth just plummeted on the tracker."

Beep.

"Three for three," said Reg. "He's locked on."

"Okay, we don't have long," said Harvey. "I'm not sure what we're up against here. I'm expecting the second taxi with another lunatic behind the wheel, but we should be ready for the cavalry. These aren't skilled killers, but they are ruthless and will do anything for the cause. They won't even need to get close to me with a car bomb."

"This is insane," said Melody. "You have no idea what they're capable of."

"No, you're right," said Harvey, "I don't. But neither do you and this way we'll find out sooner rather than later." Harvey finished stuffing all the phones into various pockets of his cargo pants. "Melody, can you set yourself up discreetly in those trees there?" Harvey pointed to a copse of trees surrounded by long wild grass.

Melody climbed out the car, retrieved her Diemaco from the boot, tapped on the car window as a gesture of good luck to Reg and Harvey, and walked away carrying the Peli case. She needed to get into position, put the rifle together and calm her breathing down.

"Reg, keep your head down, stay out of sight and shout when you see something. You get the plate numbers?"

"Yeah, I'm working on it now."

"Good you'll need them more than us, let's hope we can do this and get to them before they end up like poor old Arthur." Harvey opened his door and stepped out. "Keep the comms open," he said, then closed the door, glanced around him, turned, and walked calmly across the expanse of grass. His limp was clearly visible but much better than it had been an hour before.

Harvey walked slowly to the centre of the open land. He

saw Melody drop into the long grass five or six hundred yards to his right, and carried on walking for a minute to give Melody a chance to put the rifle together. Then he gave her another minute to calm her breathing. Emotions were high, her adrenaline would only need a little hint of action, and her heart would start pumping fast.

He glanced across at her and saw no movement. So he stopped, folded his arms, planted his feet shoulder width apart, and stood ready for whatever was about to happen.

He could have been wrong, his theory could have been way off. The whole strategy was based on assumptions which themselves were based on guesses. But what else did they have? If they waited for facts to arrive, they'd get nowhere.

Harvey stood for twenty minutes, turning every now and then to change his viewpoint. A few men walked past more than a hundred meters away. Some walked dogs, another just walked with his hands in his pockets, cutting across the grass to get somewhere. A group of teenagers sat on a bench a few hundred meters away, two on the seat, three on the back, They passed a joint between them and kept their hoods up to stay out of the wind that blew unobstructed over the patch of wild.

The wind was gusting. When it dropped, the world seemed silent, but when the gusts came, the cold wind was loud in Harvey's left ear. His right ear was protected by the ear-piece, which was silent. Even Reg wasn't making any jokes. Tensions were high in the team.

Two hours had passed when a man walked to Harvey's right alongside the lake. A casual glance told Harvey the man had a beard, was below six feet and wasn't in a hurry. He was foreign, judging by the skin tone. Harvey looked passed him but kept his eyes focused.

A taxi drove into the car park and pulled up beside the team's Audi.

"Guys," said Reg.

"Reg, did you get the plates of that taxi?" said Melody.

"I'm running them now. They belong to a blue Ford, they're stolen plates.

"Ah, Christ," said Melody.

The man with the beard was a hundred yards away from Harvey. He adjusted direction slightly and began to take a route that would lead him close to Harvey and on towards the taxi.

"You guys seeing this?" said Harvey.

"Harvey, can you take a step to your right?" said Melody. "You're blocking my view."

Harvey causally kicked the grass around him and moved three paces to his right."

The man adjusted his course, he was typing something on his phone as he walked.

"And again, Harvey, he's changed his course again."

"He knows you're there," said Harvey. "He's using me to block your shot."

The bearded man suddenly stopped and looked up from his phone. His eyes were wild, pumped full of adrenaline, fear, hate, and whatever else. Harvey could see the man's chest moving with his heavy breathing. He was thirty meters away. If he was wearing a vest, Harvey would be obliterated at that range.

"Oh, Jesus," said Reg. "I have him in the binos, he's fumbling for something in his sleeve."

"A vest?" said Melody

The taxi revved its engine. Reg kept low but adjusted his position. The taxi driver's face was obscured by a long white headscarf.

"You guys," said Reg. "This taxi's getting ready to play."

"Mr Harvey?" the man called. He brought his hands together and pulled his cuffs down over his hands.

"Reg," said Harvey. "Does beardy have anything in his hand?"

"Left looks clear, although his right hand is clenched."

"Melody, you ready for this?" asked Harvey.

"Copy. Drop on my count when the wind drops. Reg, get ready to run like hell."

"What do you want?" called Harvey to the bearded man. "Hold fire, Melody," he said under his breath.

"You've been busy," he replied,

"Not as busy as you."

"Did you honestly think that luring me out here would put you in a strong position?"

"I've seen your face now, that's the only position I need," replied Harvey.

"How is your friend?"

"My friend?" Harvey replied. "I don't have friends. You need to check your intel."

"Oh, Mr Harvey. You surely remember Arthur?"

"Name doesn't ring a bell," said Harvey. He glanced across at the taxi four hundred yards to his left. He could hear the diesel engine being revved. "Is that your mate? Sounds like he's having trouble."

"He's just fine, Mr Harvey."

"I bet he didn't do the knowledge either did he?" Harvey was referring to the extremely stringent test of London that all black cab drivers had to get through, in order to earn their right to drive a black taxi.

"That is a blessed man," said the bearded seriously. "Do not mock him."

"Guys, I'm in a spot of trouble here," said Reg over the ear-piece.

"Okay, Reggie, don't panic, I'm watching him," said Melody.

"So is he," said Reg. "He's looking right at me."

"Reg, stay focused. Have you got tabs on that tracker yet?" said Harvey quietly.

"It's coming."

"Don't play games, Mr Harvey," said beard. "We do not need to hurt your friends, but we will if we have to. I'm sure you have seen what we are capable of."

"Capable isn't the word I'd have used."

"You're going to walk towards my friend, Mr Harvey. Then you are going to sit inside the taxi."

"And where is it exactly I'm going?"

"Your destination depends on how nicely you decide to play, Mr Stone."

"If I play nicely?"

"You will see."

"If I don't play nicely?"

"Somewhere special."

"Will you be coming with me?"

"I'm ready to go to either destination, Mr Harvey. I've been ready for a very long time."

"And if I don't?"

"Your friend, Reg, isn't it? He will most certainly die."

"He's not my friend," said Harvey.

"He's not your friend?"

"That's right, he's not my friend."

"He looked like a friend this morning when you all learned about poor old Mr Denver. I watched you all, it was very touching."

"You should have joined us, we could have touched you."

"Enough of the small talk, Mr Harvey. Walk."

Harvey turned away from the man and muttered to Melody, "Melody call the distance, let me know if he closes in."

"This is crazy, Harvey, we should just take them both out."

"Too risky, Reg you have me on screen?"

"Three times."

Harvey stopped in front of the taxi and stared through the windscreen at the driver. The driver stared back grinning. His front tooth was missing. Harvey continued to stare.

"Closing in, ten metres," said Melody.

Harvey spat on the windscreen.

"Five."

The man stared back and lifted his hand. Two wires hung from his fist, and he dropped down to the floor on the passenger side. He continued to grin.

"Two metres."

"Hands on the bonnet, Mr Harvey."

"He's stopped, two paces behind you."

Harvey saw beard in the windscreens reflection.

"Listen carefully to me, Mr Harvey, you will do exactly what I say."

"Will I?" Harvey continued to stare at the driver.

"Yes, Mr Harvey, you will. Do you know what is special about this taxi?"

"It's not a blue Ford?"

"Very good, Mr Harvey, what else?"

"I'm guessing it stinks by the looks of the driver."

"The taxi is rigged with explosives, Mr Harvey, but you already knew that didn't you?"

"I had an idea."

"You're a smart man, Mr Harvey, I won't insult you with games."

"Too kind."

"Can you tell me what will happen if you do not get into the taxi?"

Harvey stared at the driver.

"What do I win if I'm right?"

"You don't win anything, I'm afraid, Mr Harvey," beard chuckled. "It's just a game."

"You said you wouldn't insult me with games."

"There is one more taxi waiting for its next fare, its final fare."

"Let me guess, it's also loaded with explosives and is parked somewhere close to a bunch of people."

"Very good, Mr Harvey, it is loaded with explosives, but it is not parked near lots of people. I would hope you think a little more of me than that. I am somewhat resourceful and, I like to think, creative too."

"I don't think anything of you. You'll just be another dead man when all this is over, and I'll be thinking about more important things. Like getting a coffee, or washing your blood off my fingers."

"Would you like me to tell you?"

"Go for it."

"You'll never guess."

Harvey didn't reply.

"Ask me for help, Mr Harvey."

Harvey didn't reply.

"Would you like to, how do you say, phone a friend?"

"I already told you I don't have friends."

"Do you think Frank will know where it is parked, the other taxi?"

Harvey didn't reply.

"You seem to have gone quiet, Mr Harvey, I was enjoying our little chat."

Harvey stared at the driver. He heard Melody over the comms talking to Reg.

"Reg, do you copy this?" she said.

"Yes, Melody, I'm piecing it together."

"Can you get onto the CCTV in HQ?"

"I'm opening the webcam of the command centre."

"Tell me what you see," said Melody. "Harvey, I have this man, clean shot, no problem."

Harvey didn't reply.

"With your left hand, Mr Harvey, using only your finger and your thumb, I want you to slowly remove your weapon and throw it on the floor."

Harvey did as instructed. He threw the Sig down on the ground, out of reach of both him and the beard.

"Good. You may now step into the vehicle."

"Can I ride up front?"

The beard chuckled again then stopped abruptly. "No, you ride in the back."

"Doesn't look very comfy, you removed all the seats."

"I'm sure you'll find a way, but please be careful, plastic explosive is quite volatile."

Harvey stepped towards the door, he caught sight of Reg who sat wide eyed in the rear of the Audi.

"Harvey, say the word and he's gone," said Melody.

"You're not going to like this," said Reg.

"Go ahead, Reg," said Melody.

"Well, there's a black taxi parked in Denver's workshop."

"As I thought," said Melody quietly.

"Some hairy guy is in my seat," said Reg.

"He's what? The tech guy?" asked Melody.

"Yeah, he's using the power of my command centre, no wonder he's one step ahead of us."

"Can you see what he's doing?"

"Not yet, I'm working on it," said Reg.

Harvey turned to the bearded man. "Before I get in, my friend drives away."

"I thought you said you didn't have any friends, Mr Harvey."

Harvey didn't reply.

"Go ahead, he's of no use to us."

"Reg," called Harvey over the taxi. Harvey saw Reg lift his

head from his laptop at the mention of his name. "Go, leave. Now."

Reg slowly opened the rear door. He took a tentative step toward the driver's door.

Harvey nodded at him. "It's fine, Reg. Go."

Reg looked across at Al Sayan, who turned to face him.

"Before you leave, Mr Reg,"

Reg had one leg in the car. He didn't reply.

"I see you met my friend," said beard. "Handsome isn't he?"

Harvey looked on proudly as Reg stared the man down and stood resolutely.

"He tells me you have quite an impressive setup. LUCY isn't it? How cute. I hope the old man is comfortable."

"What's he talking about, Reg?" said Melody over the comms.

Reg didn't reply.

"Okay, if you won't tell Mr Harvey, I will tell him."

"They have Frank," said Reg.

18

CAPTURING THE BEAST

HARVEY SAT ON THE FOLD-DOWN SEAT OF THE TAXI. HE had his back to the driver. Al Sayan sat down beside him in the adjacent fold down seat, and pulled the door closed. The taxi began to reverse, and Harvey heard the automatic locks click into place.

"You know the danger you are in, Mr Harvey?"

Harvey didn't reply.

"You are sat in a confined space with twenty-five kilos of plastic explosives, plus some other things we found."

"Other things?"

"Yes, you know, nails, screws, ball bearings. Small things. Much pain, Mr Harvey, for the man who gets too close."

"What about the innocents?"

"Innocents? Mr Harvey, I have been in this country a long, long time now and I am afraid I rarely see innocence. Ignorance, yes, I see this. But innocence? No."

"What would happen if I attacked you now?"

"If you attacked me, Mr Harvey, why would you do this? I have been polite have I not?"

"You know me?"

"I know a great deal of things, Mr Harvey. You are a very interesting man."

Harvey glanced out the window and saw they were heading back into London. He needed to buy time, he needed answers.

"Am I? You must live a very boring life if you find me interesting Mr Sayan."

"Ah, you have worked it out. My name."

"I had an idea it was you. Then I smelled you, and knew it had to be."

"You insult me, Mr Harvey? That's not playing nicely," said Al Sayan. "I have followed you with interest. I believe we have a mutual friend."

"Stimson?"

"You are highly regarded, and your history is a tragedy." Al Sayan looked pathetically at Harvey. "Your poor sister, what an awful ordeal for such a young girl to go through. Tell me, was it two men or three men, Mr Harvey, that so callously raped her?"

Harvey tensed, but Al Sayan saw the trigger and raised his hand with two wires trailing from his fist. "Ah ah ah, Mr Harvey, I must warn you." He smiled and bared his dirty brown teeth. "I must confess I am wearing a little jacket I made myself. Extra security. I'm sure you understand. If I release my grip, the vest will be detonated, the explosion will be significant on its own. But inside here? It will also detonate our little passengers." Al Sayan gestured at the long strips of PX5 that sat between the seat frames.

"It was three, wasn't it? I remember now, you always thought it was two, but then you learned of your brother's, if you do not mind me saying, unforgivable involvement in the ordeal." Al Sayan paused and studied Harvey. "How did it feel? To catch him? I heard that Donald Cartwright's body was quite literally torn apart. His throat was ripped open, his eyes ripped out and his genitals stuffed in his mouth. That's impressive, Mr Harvey.

Harvey didn't reply.

"And then there was Julios, what a man. I saw a photo of him once, and I thought to myself, wow. This man was a strong and capable man, Mr Harvey." Al Sayan leaned back onto the door behind him. "Am I right? Was he as strong and capable as he looked?"

Harvey didn't reply.

"You're not much fun, Mr Harvey. Why you don't talk?"

Harvey didn't reply.

I heard that Julios was the man who trained you, and that you were so very close. Am I right, Mr Harvey? Were you so very close?"

Harvey didn't reply.

"Ah, I am right. I can see it in your face. There is much pain in your eyes. You really are a sensitive man, Mr Harvey, surprisingly sensitive."

Harvey didn't reply.

"So if you don't want to talk about your poor sister, or your good dead friend, Julios, perhaps you'd like to talk about your parents?"

Harvey stared at Al Sayan.

"Yes, now we strike nerves, Mr Harvey. Look at the anger in you, so wild." Al Sayan leaned forward. "I cannot imagine the anger I would feel if I knew that my life had been full of so many secrets and lies, Mr Harvey. I understand your rage, truly. To have the one man you trusted and respected keep secrets from you, when you so clearly and plainly were looking under every stone you found, it must be a very difficult thing to deal with."

"I didn't trust or respect him, we had an arrangement. So think what you like. Are we nearly there? I'm getting tired of this."

"Ah, Mr Harvey, I do seem to have touched on something sensitive. You cannot avoid talking about it. In fact, talking is sometimes the best way to overcome your anger. Humour me, Mr Harvey."

Harvey didn't reply.

"So you didn't respect him or trust him, yet he was your best friend? I find that hard to believe, Mr Harvey."

"John wasn't my best friend," said Harvey. "He was my foster father and my boss. That's as far as the relationship went."

"Oh, Mr Harvey. I am not talking of John Cartwright. Oh, no. I am talking of Mr Julios, of course. He was your mentor, am I right? He trained you?"

"Yeah, he taught me a few things."

Al Sayan laughed. " A few things? You are a master, Mr Harvey, a dangerous man. You were carved by Julios like a sculptor carves a stone statue. He chips away at the stone, one tiny piece at a time." Al Sayan flicked Harvey's shoulder lightly. "Then he will stand back and admire his work, he will check the balance of his creation, and maybe chip a tiny piece off from this side." Al Sayan touched Harvey's cheek.

"You getting dangerously close," said Harvey.

"I am merely describing how Julios, your mentor, your best friend, your sculptor carved you, shaped you, created you. Stone from Stone, Mr Harvey."

Harvey didn't reply. He took a deep breath through his nose.

"That's right, Mr Harvey, control your breathing. Let the anger flow through you, not out of you. Just as Julios taught you."

Harvey didn't reply, he stared at the plastic explosives in a row.

"So it must have destroyed you when you learned of your sculptor's treachery?"

The squeal of brakes as the taxi slowed for traffic lights was loud in the back. Harvey rocked in his seat.

"Do you think he would have done it if he knew?" said Al Sayan. "Do you think that if he had known what a great and dangerous stone statue he would create, he would still have killed them, Mr Harvey?"

Harvey didn't reply.

"Do you think he savoured the moment? When he stood over your mother and father? Do you think he regretted it afterwards?" Al Sayan laughed out loud.

Harvey pushed up with his legs and held Al Sayan against the glass with his forearm. Harvey brought his head back and smashed his forehead into the man's face. The driver broke, and Harvey lost his balance, he stumbled and fell against the glass partition. Al Sayan shoved him back to his seat and held his face with one hand. Blood ran from his nose through his fingers. Al Sayan nodded to the driver, and the taxi drove on.

Harvey was limp in his seat. His mind swam, confused, dizzied with memories of Julios standing over his faceless parents. The kind smiles and nurturing on Julios face as Harvey swam in the pool, and Julios lifted him out as a young boy. The moments they had shared after a sparring session, when they had both laid on their backs on the rubber mats in John's gym, panting and sweating. The times Harvey had discussed his efforts at finding his parents' killer. Each time, his mind came back to Julios' huge frame standing over his dead parents.

"How does it feel, Mr Harvey?"

Silence.

"Perhaps you need some time to consider what you just learned."

Harvey sat with his arms resting on his knees. He stared at the grooves in the wooden floor of the taxi. His heart was racing, he needed air.

"We are here," said Al Sayan.

Harvey felt the taxi slow and turn sharply to the left. He looked up out the window and saw the Stratford warehouse on his right. The driver got out, and a few minutes later the sliding shutter door screeched open. Then the taxi pulled inside, and the shutter door slammed shut. The locks on the doors popped open when the driver hit the switch in the cab, and Al Sayan stepped out but kept his eye on Harvey. Harvey was limp and despondent.

"Out you come, Mr Harvey, we have a tight schedule."

Harvey didn't reply. He didn't move.

The driver opened the door on Harvey's side and pulled two plastic zip ties on Harvey's wrists, binding them together. Harvey stepped out and took in his surroundings. The warehouse looked gloomy even in the daytime. The weak strip lights that hung from thin chains left the sides and corners of the space in shadow. The pile of seats still sat under the tarp, and the wheels were still stacked in the corner with the car jack. The large wooden box had been removed. A plastic tarp was pulled out flat behind the old forklift. It was three metres square, and on it stood a tripod and a video camera.

"You've been here before, Mr Harvey, we found your little listening devices." He tutted. "Such devious behaviour. Did you honestly think that I am a caveman? I think you will find that we are far more sophisticated than you give us credit for, Mr Harvey." Al Sayan walked away towards the back of the warehouse. "Follow me, Mr Harvey, I'm sure I don't need to prompt you anymore."

Al Sayan stopped at the far end of the warehouse and opened the door to a small dark room. "I hope you will find it comfortable in here. I'm afraid the building just isn't as equipped as I would like it to be, but it is only temporary."

Harvey felt the gun in his back. The driver stood behind him. Harvey smelled his warm, stale breath. He stepped forward. Rooms ran the length of the right-hand side of the warehouse. The walls of each room were built from thick concrete blocks, and the doors were of thick wood with metal plates fixed front and back as reinforcement. There were four identical rooms in total. The first was open. Harvey glanced inside as he walked past, roughly eight foot by eight foot with no window. He presumed the other rooms would all be the same.

The next room along was closed, as was the third. Al Sayan held the door to room four open for Harvey.

"Goodbye, for now, Mr Harvey. Perhaps one day we will meet again."

"Leaving so soon?" replied Harvey.

"I'm afraid I'm a workaholic. My friend here has a pressing engagement to keep. He is about to change the face of London." Al Sayan smiled cruelly. "You're witnessing history, Mr Harvey."

Harvey didn't reply. Instead, he took a deep breath through his nose and stepped into the cell.

"I would urge you to leave any thoughts of escape to one side. You're a smart man, Mr Harvey, I'm sure you have worked out that our little garage here has been suitably prepared. It will be several days before they find any of your remains."

The door slammed shut, and a series of locks and bolts clicked and slotted into place.

A silence fell in the dark room. Harvey could barely make out the door. He stood for a moment, then began to plan.

He heard the shutter doors open at the far end of the warehouse. The taxi's diesel engine started and the shutters closed again.

Harvey mulled over what Al Sayan had said. Over and over, Al Sayan's words repeated in his mind. How true was it? How had he known about Hannah? He'd saved the final blow until they'd arrived at the warehouse. Al Sayan had known the news of Julios would knock Harvey for six, but he still couldn't believe it, didn't believe him. Yet he knew deep down that it was true.

It made sense. Harvey's attempts at understanding had been blocked time after time, downplayed almost. Even Julios had known something, and steered any conversation of his parents, away to something else. Harvey thought back to the last conversation he'd had with Julios. They'd been buying a van load of automatic rifles from the Thomsons and had been waiting at the spot. Julios had made a mistake, he let slip that he'd known something, then brushed it off.

Harvey sank to the cold stone floor. He leaned against the wall and brought his knees up to his chest. He pulled his bound wrists over his knees and buried his face in his legs.

Being alone was something that Harvey was used to. Even if he had chosen a career in an office, doing some mundane, ordinary job, he'd still be the same. His very nature made Harvey a solitary person. But he'd always had one friend. For most of his childhood that friend had been Hannah. Julios had been in the background and was friendly, but his one true friend had always been Hannah. She'd never let him down. Then, when she'd died, Julios stepped in.

Was it because Julios felt guilty? Was that it? Was that why Julios had suddenly became so involved in Harvey's life? Did he pity Harvey? He didn't need pitying, he was Harvey Stone. He was strong and resilient. He pulled a boot lace from his tan boots. Then, in the darkness, he tied a large loop in both ends of the long cord.

He didn't need friends. He was Harvey Stone.

He pulled the lace through the two zip-ties on his wrists.

So what if Julios had lied? His whole life had been a charade anyway. People had watched him try to understand

and fail for as long as he could remember. What was the point in trying to understand now?

He pulled a loop over each boot.

So what if I'm alone. Don't they know who I am?.

He leaned back and lifted his legs, working his feet back and forth, the lace heating and wearing through the plastic zip-ties.

Al Sayan can't stop me with words. I'm Harvey Stone.

The lace cut through the first zip-tie.

I'm Harvey Stone.

Snap.

The second zip tie fell to the floor. Harvey replaced his bootlace, rubbed his wrists and stood up.

"Come on then, Harvey Stone. Since when did a closed door stop you?"

He stood and stretched. He closed his eyes to the darkness and breathed calm, deep breaths. He filled his lungs with the stale air and pictured the room before Al Sayan had closed and locked the door.

Breeze block walls, hard and thick. Solid wooden door with steel reinforcement in the form of a plate on each side of the door. The wooden frame. Harvey imagined the frame being screwed into the concrete blocks; strong but not impossible to shear off.

He walked towards the wall with the door and felt along until he found the wooden frame. His hands felt the wood in the darkness. He touched the door handle, cool in the cold warehouse.

Then he felt the hinges on the weakest side. He had heard the many bolts being slid into place into recesses drilled into the concrete blocks. The hinges, however, would just be drilled into the door frame.

He stepped back with his left leg. It still throbbed, and Harvey knew without looking that it would be badly bruised.

He'd been lucky, the taxi had been empty, and had bounced over his leg. The tissue would be damaged, the muscles sore, but the bone was intact. It just needed time to heal.

Harvey slowly raised his right foot to the hinged side of the door and judged a solid kick with the heel of his boot.

He lowered his foot, stepped back and kicked.

Thud.

It was solid.

Thud. Thud.

He thought of the taxi making its way into the city.

Thud.

He heard a small shower of dust fall from the concrete blocks surrounding the door frame.

Thud. Thud.

The taxi driver's dirty, toothless grin.

Thud.

The wires that ran from the plastic explosives in the rear.

Thud.

People crossing the street, stepping back to take photos of St Paul's to show their families when they got home.

Thud.

Ordinary people wearing ordinary clothes going to ordinary jobs.

Thud. Thud.

More dust.

Al Sayan.

Thud.

His cruel smile.

Thud.

Julios.

Thud, thud, thud.

Standing over his dead parents.

Crack.

The lies.

Crack.

The explosion.

The door frame split at the top and light spilt into the small room.

Thud.

More light.

Thud.

I don't need anybody.

Crack.

Julios.

Crack.

Al Sayan.

Crunch. The door fell away. Its lower hinge held true but twisted under the weight of the wood and steel plate.

Harvey stood, closed his eyes, took a deep breath and stepped out into the warehouse.

Dust had filled the air from the crashing and banging and it hung in swirling beams of light from the extractor fan that span slowly in the centre of the warehouse's rear wall.

Everything else remained as it had. Harvey strode towards the two exit doors. The shutter had been pulled down over the single door. A small repair job had been done, and Harvey saw the new wood where he had broken the door with Melody.

The large sliding shutter doors were locked, but Harvey had a plan.

He passed the other rooms and noted the locks. He stepped back to room three and put his ear to the door.

He knocked.

Nothing.

He knocked again, slightly harder.

Then faintly, he heard a voice. "Hello?"

19

GENTLE GIANT

MELODY WATCHED THE TAXI LEAVE THE CAR PARK, THEN popped up to her feet, grabbed the rifle and the Peli case, and ran to the Audi. Reg moved out the driver's seat and climbed back into the rear. Melody snatched open the boot, dumped the Peli case inside and carried the rifle to the passenger seat. She made the rifle safe, then set it down and wedged it between the seat and the door so it wouldn't move.

"How's HQ looking?" she asked, "How many do we have there?"

She slammed the car into reverse and accelerated through the empty car park.

"Melody?" said Reg, looking out the rear window with concern on his face.

"Talk to me, Reg. What's HQ looking like?"

She slammed on the brakes and spun the wheel, dipped the clutch, and found first gear. As she slammed the accelerator down once again, the car spun and its momentum from the spin and power from first gear sent the rear wheels sliding out across the gravel. Small stones pounded the bodywork and the underside of the car.

"Reg, come on." She accelerated away from the car park and settled in for the ride, pulling her belt on and checking her mirrors.

"The taxi went the other way, Melody," said Reg.

"Harvey will have to look after himself. Headquarters?"

"I'm looking at my webcam, there's only one man there as far as I can see.

Melody took a final glance in her rearview mirror and saw the taxi disappear from sight. "Good luck, Harvey."

Reg heard her, and glance behind him. "You think he'll be okay?"

Melody sighed. "I don't know, Reg. We need to get Frank."

"I'm looking at Frank now. He's tougher than he looks."

"He's been through enough."

"I honestly have no idea how I'd react if that were me." Reg stared at the image. Frank was sat behind the man at Reg's computers. He was gagged and tied to a chair. It was the chair from Harvey's desk. His legs were bound, and his wrists were tied behind him.

"I saw you back there, Reg," said Melody. "You held your own."

"The driver though," said Reg. "What the hell goes through these people's minds? He looked crazy. *Surely* they feel *some* kind of remorse? He was pure evil."

"It's exactly as Frank said, Reg."

"What?"

"It's what we're up against. There's no respect for life."

"This is too big for us, Melody, we need to call it in."

"Call it in? What do you think will happen, Reg? I'll tell you, the taxi won't be stopped and the driver won't be arrested, he'll detonate the car. And Frank? They'll detonate that taxi too. We can do this, Reg. What would Harvey do?"

"Normally? Torture them or something."

"No, he wouldn't, you talk about him like he's a monster, Reg. He'd wait, then he'd make a plan, and then he'd execute."

"We don't have time to wait. Do you have a plan, Melody?"

"Are you controlling LUCY?"

"Not controlling, observing. If I make a move, he'll know I'm there and kick me out."

"That's good, stay out of sight, but watch him."

"What are you going to do? We can't go kicking the doors down and storming in."

"We have to believe that Harvey will be okay, and if Harvey's okay, that means he'll take care of the taxi. Our focus is Frank, HQ and the other taxi. Pull up the satellite of HQ and find me a roof."

"A roof?"

"Somewhere I can get a shot in."

"Okay, there's flats in the next road, but-"

"Can we get on top?"

"I guess so, but-"

"That's all we need. If Harvey takes his taxi out, they'll need the one in HQ to do the job. We can take them out from the roof. It's a gamble, but if I can make the shot-"

"Oh no," said Reg.

"Tell me, Reg."

"I'm watching him. He's smart. He's taken control of the CCTV in the city."

"How's he done that?" asked Melody.

"He's into the Bishopsgate control centre. That's where the police monitor the city cameras from."

"What's he looking at?"

"Looks like Queen Victoria Street. Have a guess where?"

"The auction house?"

"White van parked outside. Crew of workman beside it."

"The buddha."

"To be honest, they can take the buddha, I don't care anymore."

"Reg, come on, we need to focus on the taxis."

"There's only two of us, Melody. Denver's gone, Harvey's been captured, and Frank is tied up next to a ticking time bomb."

"Reg, stop it," said Melody harshly. "You're the best god damn tech guy I know. Think clearly, what can we do? I'll tell you what we can do, one thing at a time. That's what we can do. That's all we *can* do."

"One thing at a time."

"One thing at a time, Reg," replied Melody,

"Right, time to get LUCY back," said Reg.

"What are you going to do?"

"I'm going to show this bastard exactly how powerful LUCY is."

Reg began to type frantically on the laptop.

"First of all, I need to get him off of her."

"What are you doing, Reg?"

"I'm logging on to LUCY's admin console and disabling his phone to start with. He won't know until he tries to use it."

Melody looked in the rearview mirror and saw Reg with the tip of his tongue between his lips, concentrating.

"Right, now let's freak him out a little,"

"What you got in mind?"

"Just ringing a few phones around the building. The digital phone system has a test feature that can ring all the phones at once. I'm even setting the ringtone to Rule Britannia, boom, there, now he's wondering what's going on."

"Don't piss him off, Reg, we don't want him to detonate."

"I'm just toying with him. If he's any kind of specialist, he'll try to resist me before it comes to that."

"Okay, if you're sure."

"I'm sure, Melody. There we go, his account is disabled, and his screen is locked. From LUCY's admin console I can capture his keystrokes."

"What will that do?"

"That'll enable me to get his password, so I can undo whatever damage he's done once we're done with him. He'll likely be trying to access the system, so LUCY will capture everything he does. I can also pull a report on everywhere he's been in the system with that user account."

Reg hummed to himself, a sign he was pleased with his efforts.

"Right, next, remove the trackers from our phones, they're all in Harvey's pockets right now, but he may have given another system access."

"We're nearly there, Reg."

"I'm nearly done, I'm just going to shut the screens down, and then..." Reg hit the keyboard with finality. "Turn the lights off."

"Nice touch, have you ever seen how dark it is in there with the lights off?"

"Yeah it's creepy,"

"Is that the road there?" Melody pointed to a side road close to the HQ turning.

"That's the one, the flats are at the end on the left."

Melody stopped the car outside the flats on double yellow lines.

She grabbed the rifle and the magazine from the passenger side, climbed out and slammed the door shut.

Reg opened his door.

"Stay there Reg. I need eyes."

Reg pointed to his ear-piece and cupped his hand around his ear. "If you use the comms this close, he'll hear, use code."

Melody was aware that she was standing in the middle of a road with an automatic rifle. It was a dead-end side street that led down to the river, so it was quiet, but people still had windows.

"Before you do anything, Melody," began Reg, "I'm taking my LUCY back."

"I'll give two clicks on the ear-piece, Reg. On the first one, I want you to sound the alarms in the building."

"Copy." Reg was listening intently and realised the plan as Melody explained her requests.

"Second time, I want you to open the shutter doors. I'll take care of the rest."

She turned and saw a teenager run from the flats and disappear around the back of the building. Clean white trainers, tracksuit bottoms and a thick hooded sweater; it was probably a paranoid drug dealer that happened to see Melody out his window. Melody caught the door as it slowly swung shut and took the stairs. The flats were low rise, five stories. She ran all the way up and kicked through the door at the top. Pigeons scurried away in a chaotic bid for escape. The roof was covered in gravel, bird droppings and aerials. She sank to the floor and crawled across the stones and crap to the low wall that faced HQ.

She chanced a glance over the wall. To HQ, it was a six hundred yard shot, not easy with the wind off the river below. She was protected by the walls so couldn't feel the wind, but the trees and clothes that hung from washing lines further along the road told her it was gusting still, and quite strong. Five or six knots. She'd need to time her shot right.

She brought the rifle up and sat the fold-down bi-pod on the wall, then pulled the rifle butt into her shoulder and stood until the green metal shutter doors of HQ came into view through the scope.

She was relying on human instinct. She was relying on gut feeling. She was relying on hope.

Melody clicked once on her ear-piece.

A piercing alarm sounded from the building. The flashing light above the doors began to spin and cast an orange glow even in the daylight. The alarm sound would be deafening inside. Melody remembered that when it was installed, they all had to leave the building; the noise was intolerable.

She clicked a second time.

The shutter doors cracked open then, as the motor took up the slack in the concertina doors, they slowly dragged open. Melody imagined the man inside holding his ears, then trying to find the door override, a large red button on one side of the shutters. The door was open more than a metre now.

Melody calmed her breathing. Her focus through the scope was in the centre of the gap in the shutter door. The noise of the alarm was loud, even from six-hundred yards away. Nothing.

"Come on, you bastard. Show yourself."

Then a foot appeared in the scope's magnified view.

It shuffled sideways. Black business shoes and black suit trousers. Frank. Behind him was Al Sayan's tech guy.

Melody lowered the butt of the rifle a fraction and saw Frank, gagged and blindfolded, his hands behind his back. The man was standing behind him with his arm around Franks' neck, pushing him towards the shutter door.

The Arab stood directly behind Frank. There was no clear shot for Melody.

Melody kept Frank's head in view, knowing that the terrorist's face was just behind. She just needed Frank to move, but the other man was cautious or afraid. Determined.

The door stopped moving when the Afghan hit the big red button. One more push began its closing action. Melody's heart raced as the door slowly crept into view from the right-hand side of her scope.

Frank, whose ankles had been untied to walk him to the

door, suddenly bent forward and slammed his head back into the man's face, then bent double all the way down. The terrorist was caught off guard and brought this hands up to his bloodied nose.

Time stood still.

Melody opened her free eye and saw the trees still. The bright white shirt that hung out to dry hung freely and motionless. Melody squeezed the trigger, and before the man's hands reached his ruined nose, the back of his head exploded in a shower of bone, blood and brains.

Frank fell to the floor and was still, blinded by the rags the man had tied around his head.

"Kill the noise, Reg," said Melody. "Target is down."

The alarms fell silent.

"Open the doors."

The shutter doors began their slow opening action. The electronic motors pulled on long chains, winding them onto the chain spools. The light filled the floor of headquarters. Melody could see Denver's workshop area. The taxi, the blood. The pristine tool chests and workbench, the dead man on the floor.

"That was for you, Denver buddy."

20

THE ANGEL AND THE BEAST

HARVEY FOUND A LONG CROWBAR, AND AFTER A FEW minutes had successfully ripped the door off room three. He stepped to one side and let the door fall to the floor, then stepped into the empty doorway.

The room was the same as the one he'd been locked in. No furniture or shelving around the edges, no windows and a dirty, dusty concrete floor. The only difference was the chair that stood in the centre of the room. Sat on the chair was a small girl. Her long, blonde hair hung across her eyes. She'd been unable to move the chair because her hands were tied, as were her ankles. She wasn't gagged or blindfolded, but there was no reason to in the small dark room.

Harvey saw the dirty face that stared up at her, scared and trembling. She had cried so much that her eyes were puffed. Dried tear marks ran down her face, and cut through the grime like water on the walls of a limestone cave. Two eyes shone from swollen eyelids, big and blue.

No words were needed.

Harvey stepped closer with his hands held up in a gesture of peace. He bent down to untie her, but she fought and struggled. Harvey didn't bother to try and calm her, he would untie her and then she would calm down. She struggled the whole time, and when he had finished, she sat still.

"My name's Harvey," he said. "I'm going to get you back to your mum. Would you like that?"

The girl nodded.

"Okay, let's get out of here. I don't like it here at all, do you?"

The girl looked up at him with her big eyes and shook her head.

"What's your name?"

The girl didn't reply.

"That's okay, you don't have to tell me, but let's go somewhere safe."

He held out his hand, which she took before slipping off the old wooden chair to the floor.

They walked to the large shutter door that the taxi had used.

"I need to find a way to open the door. Will you help me and stay there, while I have a look around?"

The girl nodded and hugged her arms around herself.

"Good girl, I'll just be here, I won't leave you." Harvey stepped across to the big pile of junk by the seats that had been ripped out the taxi.

He stepped back, and bumped into the girl.

"Hey, I thought I asked you to stay by the door?"

The girl didn't reply.

"That's okay, we can look together." He took her hand. "We're looking for something long and strong." Then he saw it, an old scaffold tube leaned up against the wall. Harvey bent down, picked the girl up and sat her on his hip. He stepped over the junk, car parts, gearboxes and heavy tools, grabbed the scaffold tube with one hand and walked back to the shutter doors. He set the girl down a few meters from the door. "This is going to be a bit noisy so put your fingers in your ears like this." He motioned putting fingers in his ears and squinted his eyes shut.

The scaffold tube was two feet long. He turned to face the doors and pulled the tube back behind him. Then, before he swung, he gave her a quick look. "Are you ready?"

She nodded.

Harvey launched into an attack on the bottom part of the door and wedged the tube between the main unit and the smaller leaf section. Once he had the end of the tube through, he used his weight to lever the door open at the bottom. The mounts broke one by one, and the bottom corner began to open outwards. Once it was open enough, he turned to the girl.

"Are you ready to get out?" He held his hand out to her.

She nodded.

"You're a brave girl," he said. "That's it, just climb through there." He lowered himself down and looked up at her. She looked down at him. "You be sure to tell me if anybody comes, okay?"

She nodded.

Harvey picked up an old screwdriver from the floor, laid down and pushed his arms through the hole. His head followed, and he wriggled until his hips caught the side of the doors. He had to pull and squeeze himself through, and the metal scraped the skin on his hips. Eventually he broke through, pulled his legs out, and rolled to stand beside her.

"See, easy," he said with a smile.

She looked up at him and lifted her arms to be carried.

"Let's go see about finding your mum eh?" he said. "Are you going to tell me your name?"

The girl rubbed her eyes then held on to his t-shirt. "Angel," she said in a soft, girly voice.

"Angel?"

She nodded.

"That's a pretty name for a pretty girl."

She buried her face into his shoulder.

"Okay, let's go. We need to find a car though, Angel," said Harvey. "Which one do you like?" Harvey pointed to the two oldest cars he could see. "Do you like the blue one or the black one?"

Angel pointed at the blue one, it was an old Ford with rusted bodywork and missing number plates. The bonnet was a lighter shade of blue than the rest of the bodywork, as if it had been replaced at some point.

The car was parked beside a van with flat tyres, and hidden from passers-by. Harvey pulled the scaffold tube through the bent shutter door and walked to the old Ford. He set the girl down and tried the door handle. It was locked. Harvey worked his fingers into the top of the driver's window and forced the glass down as much as he could. Older cars without electric windows worked on a mechanism. The winder mechanism wound a belt that raised or lowered the frame that the glass sat on. Harvey knew that the belts on old cars had slack in them from years of use, especially the driver's door. The window had dropped an inch, it wasn't enough to even get the girls arm inside.

He looked around and found a wooden wedge behind the wheel of the van. He used the scaffold tube to force the wedge out from beneath the tyre and prised the top of the driver's door open enough to slot the scaffold tube inside. Any further and he risked breaking the glass. He asked Angel to help him. She put her arm in and pulled the lock up.

"Good girl, that's a great job," he told her. She looked proud that she'd helped.

Again, Harvey tried the door, and it opened.

Next, he smashed the plastic cover beneath the steering wheel and tore it off, exposing the ignition barrel. He snapped off the barrel using the scaffold tube, leaving him with a square hole. Harvey put the flathead screwdriver from the garage into the hole and turned until the ignition lights came on, but the engine didn't turn over.

He dropped the handbrake and lowered the window. The car had a clear run of twenty meters in front of it. Harvey rocked the car back and forth. It didn't feel like it had sat there for long, the starter motor had probably died and was sat outside to be repaired. Harvey glanced at the black Vauxhall and thought it probably worked fine, was unlocked with the keys in it, but Angel had chosen the blue car.

He climbed out the car, and held the door frame. Grunting, he gave the car a push to start it in motion then ran harder and faster. He worked up a quick run of short steps, jumped into the driver's seat mid-run, selected first gear and bump started the little Ford.

He didn't brake in time and crashed the front of the car into the large bins outside the warehouse. He dipped the clutch, gave it some more gas then reversed up alongside Angel.

Harvey leaned across and opened the door for her. "How did you like that then, Angel?"

She laughed. "You crashed."

"Yeah yeah, you need to get in the back and put your belt on, okay?"

She climbed in and crawled between the front seats to sit on the back.

"You set?" He turned, she nodded. Her head barely reached the top of the glass, she would probably need a child seat, but that was the least of his worries. "Okay, let's go find your mum, then shall we?"

He pulled off and turned out of the compound. He worked the old car up to fourth gear quickly and relaxed into the drive. The little motor felt ancient compared to the team's Audi, but needs must. He considered dropping Angel at a police station, but the possible consequences were entirely unknown. He couldn't risk the delay. She'd have to go with him to London. With any luck, Melody would be there and would know what to do.

The A12 led Harvey from Stratford into the city and the steering wheel wobbled all the way. Harvey felt like the wheels would fall off at any moment. He checked in the back infrequently and Angel seemed content looking out the window at the sky and buildings that went passed.

"So, what did you say your mummy's name was?"

Angel didn't reply.

"Do you know where you live?"

She shook her head.

"That's okay, we can find a policeman who can help us. Would you like that?"

Angel nodded her head and looked back out the window.

Harvey considered his predicament. He was in a stolen car with someone's kid. His team had fallen apart, one was dead, another kidnapped and the two functional members could be just about anywhere.

He needed to find the taxi, he needed to stop the bomb, and he needed to get the kid to her parents, plus prevent the buddha being stolen, but that was way down his list.

He found his way onto the highway into London. It was a slower route that bypassed the iron circle protecting the City of London, which was manned by police twenty-four seven.

He passed the Tower of London and found Upper Thames Street. From there, he turned into the side street where Hague had run. Harvey ditched the car and took Angel in his arms.

"Okay, Angel we're going to run now."

Harvey ran to the pedestrian crossing and hit the button to cross. Normally, he would have just run across the road between cars, but he was very conscious of carrying some-body else's kidnapped kid. He crossed the road and ran up a side street in the direction of St Paul's. Then it dawned on him that he was running toward a potential bomb carrying a young girl. The odds were stacked heavily against him.

There was a sandwich shop on the side of the road. He considered taking her inside and asking the owner to take care of her, but this was London. It wasn't an option; the police would arrive in seconds. He'd taken responsibility for her and would have to deal with it.

"Okay, Angel, we're going to see some people, and I need you to stay with me okay?"

Harvey made a plan. If a cop came along, he would just say he found Angel walking the streets and hand her over. He didn't want her to be hurt, but a lot more people might die if he didn't stop the taxi.

He stood on the corner of Queen Victoria Street and Peter's Hill then turned to look about him. The auction house was around the corner, he couldn't walk any further without passing it and potentially being recognised. And he definitely couldn't do that with Angel.

He scanned the cars that drove past for the taxi. He was concentrating so hard on trying to see it that when the Volvo stopped beside him, he barely recognised Reg and Frank.

"Stone, what the-"

"Long story, Frank." Harvey bent down and looked through to Reg at the wheel. "Where's Melody?"

"Getting set up on the roof behind you. She watched you walk up from Upper Thames Street and got us on the comms."

Harvey opened the rear door and put Angel inside.

"Angel, these two men will take care of you. They're policemen, so you'll be safe, okay?"

"No, they don't look like policemen."

"Do you trust me?" he asked.

The girl hesitated then nodded.

"Okay, good girl. I need you to be grown up now, be strong for me. The man with the grey hair here is called Frank, he's a very important policeman. You can ask him all sorts of questions."

"I don't want you to go," cried Angel.

"I'm sorry I have to, but I'll be back." He closed the rear door and turned back to Frank and Reg. "You got an ear-piece for me?"

"You're in luck, Harvey," said Reg and he handed over the little ear-piece. Harvey placed it inside his ear. He hadn't liked them at first, but over the year he'd been working with the team, he'd gotten used to wearing them.

"You might need this as well, Stone." Frank handed him his Sig. Harvey discreetly checked the chamber and the magazine.

"What's the deal here?" said Harvey. "Last I heard you weren't doing so well."

"Headquarters is secured, the taxi has been disarmed, and Reg has LUCY under control again."

"So there's one taxi left?" asked Harvey.

"We believe so," replied Frank. "You've been busy." Frank gestured at the girl in the back of the Volvo.

"So have you, looks like a hell of a tea party."

"You should see the mess we made. Do we know the mother?"

"Not sure about the mother, but something tells me she's linked to all this. Reg are you tracking the taxi?" asked Harvey.

"Yeah, it stopped for a while at a mosque in Bow. They've been on the move for twenty minutes, currently working their way through the city, ETA six minutes."

"Direction?"

"Westbound. Melody is watching Cannon Street with her Diemaco."

Harvey stuck the weapon in his waist band under his t-shirt. "And the heist? Stimson?"

"Larson and a team of men are around the corner waiting for the explosion. If we hit them now, Al Sayan might be watching. LUCY ran some calculations. If the blast of twenty-five kilos of PX5 goes off right outside the cathedral, the surrounding buildings and the cathedral itself will be destroyed, but the auction house will be fairly well protected. It might lose a few windows, but Stimson will have a getaway on the chaos."

"And the priceless buddha?"

"Not if we're quick," said Frank. "I want you in position ready to take them down as soon as Melody takes the taxi out."

"Welcome back, Harvey," said Melody over the comms.

"I hear you need a hand?" replied Harvey.

"I can handle it, but if you want to come and have some fun, you're welcome."

"Shout when you take the shot. If you miss, I guess we'll all know about it."

"If I miss and it detonates, I'll be toast."

There was a silence as the team all thought about Denver.

"Yeah, well," said Harvey. "That's not going to happen."

"One minute," announced Reg.

"Get her out of here," said Harvey to Reg, then ran off, ready to slip around the corner.

"I have the driver in my sight," said Melody coolly. Harvey pictured her with one eye closed and her finger resting on the trigger. She'd be beginning to work the trigger into the crook of her index finger.

"Hold on, there's two of them," said Melody. "They've stopped, and the passenger has got out. He's walking towards the auction house on your side of the street, hundred yards."

"Al Sayan," said Harvey. "He's a decoy, where's he gone?"

"I can't see him, he's between the buildings."

Harvey ran to Cannon Street. St Paul's loomed above him. He turned right and scanned the pathways for Al Sayan. The taxi stood at the end of the road, parked as if it was waiting for a fare.

"I have the driver in my sight. Am I taking him down or what?" said Melody.

Harvey didn't reply.

"Harvey, talk to me," said Melody, keeping her voice calm and her breathing relaxed.

Just then, Harvey heard screaming coming from his left. He looked across the road at St Paul's and saw smoke pouring through the open door of a pub on Cheapside, the road that ran behind the cathedral.

People ran from coffee shops to get clear of any blast that would follow the smoke. A car swerved to the other side of the road when the driver saw people running, and slammed into a young couple who were running away. Crowds came running down towards Harvey. They ran in the road, on the pavement and across the grass, anyway they could to get away from the scene.

"Kill zone, Melody. Same as Canary Wharf."

"Where's Al Sayan?" asked Melody.

"He's disappeared," replied Harvey,

"Okay, Harvey, taxi is moving."

Harvey watched as the taxi pulled slowly out from the lay-by, and drove directly towards him.

"Take him down, Melody." Harvey ran towards the taxi. If Melody only wounded the driver, he could still hit the switch. Harvey pulled his Sig as he ran. The driver saw Harvey and accelerated. "Anytime, Melody."

"I don't have a shot," Melody replied.

Harvey stopped on the road with one hundred yards to go and aimed his Sig with two hands. He calmed his breathing and fired. The windscreen shattered, but the taxi carried on accelerating.

Fifty yards.

Harvey began to see the driver's face.

He fired his weapon again, and Harvey saw the man lurch into the back of the seat. The taxi rolled to a stop twenty meters from Harvey. If it detonated, he would be torn to pieces along with the dozens of people that were still running from the smoking pub across the street.

Harvey stepped forward slowly. With each step, Harvey kept his gun on the man. More people ran from the smoke, saw Harvey standing with a gun and stopped. A group was forming. Harvey glanced across at them. "Move, go, run." He couldn't form a sentence.

He turned back to the driver just as his head began to move, then his face caved in. Harvey heard the report of Melody's rifle, and again. The man's chest opened up from the 7.62 calibre Diemaco almost instantly.

Harvey stepped to the side of the car and wrenched the door open. The man had his hand on the switch, but would never be able to push the button or anything else again. Harvey carefully pulled the switch from his hand and laid it on the seat. Then he dragged the ruined body from the taxi. He stepped away backwards as he saw policemen running toward him. Sirens grew louder from all directions.

"Target is down," said Harvey. "We've lost Al Sayan."

21

THE SERPENT'S TRAP

"THE AUCTION HOUSE," SAID MELODY.

Harvey turned and ran along the narrow lane between the buildings opposite the cathedral. The auction house was a single five-story brick building that was surrounded on all four sides by smaller lanes. It had an industrial look and was rounded by offices buildings, coffee shops and small restaurants. It had two basement levels, a little loading bay and a modest reception. Harvey stood in front of the reception. He doubted Stimson and his men would use the main entrance, they would be behind the building.

Harvey checked the doors anyway, they were locked. He walked around the side of the auction house, turned the corner and saw the front end of the white van sticking out. He put his weapon away and pulled his t-shirt over it, then pulled out one of the phones and pretended to be typing a message while he walked.

He turned the corner by the van, expecting to be confronted by Stimson's men, but it was empty. The van was locked. A small set of steps led down to a service entrance of the building. The door was ajar.

Harvey put the phone away. If he walked in, they'd be no pretending.

"Harvey, where are you? I'm at ground level," said Melody over the comms.

"Service entrance, back side."

He stepped slowly down the steps and opened the door fully. He saw that the biometric security panel had been shorted and the double doors had been forced in.

A small corridor, ten meters long, was in front of him. It led to a T. He walked to the end and drew his weapon again, looking both ways. To the right, a set of concrete stairs led down, and a small ancient elevator with black wrought iron gates sat beside it. To the left was a series of room entrances and one large set of doors. Harvey guessed the double doors led to the rear of the auction house back stage, and the other doors were perhaps storage rooms or offices.

Harvey turned right and stood at the top of the stairs. He peered down. He could see two floors below between the iron bannister. The lowest floor was lit dimly by a yellowish glow. Harvey began the walk down the steps, slowly and quietly, as Julios had taught him all those years ago. He kept to the shadows where possible. The first floor was clear. But as he stepped onto the stairs that led to basement two, he heard the faint muffled sound of men's voices.

He checked back up the stairs, he was still alone.

He stepped to the concrete floor of basement two and into the yellow light. Another biometric panel had its wires pulled from the bottom of the unit on the wall. The lights on the security panel were off.

The lights that lit the dark corridor were a string of bulbs fixed to the ceiling beside the wall. They cast two or three shadows of Harvey as he made his way along. The walls were tiled like an old underground station. The white tiles took a yellowish glow from the dim lights above, and every sound he made was echoed in the still space.

There was only one set of doors at the end of the corridor. They were large windowless double doors, with yet another biometric panel and three heavy duty locks at the top, middle and bottom. The doors opened outwards judging by the closers, so Harvey stepped to one side and listened. He waited a full minute, another of Julios' lessons.

The voices he'd heard were clearer now, but still hushed and urgent.

"Stimson just messaged me, go go go."

"Okay, I'm going as quick as I can."

"We should have been in and out by now, what's taking so long?"

"You can't rush this, Lucas. If this doesn't go right, it'll be all bang and no buddha, know what I mean?"

"If you don't get it right, all bang and no buddha will be written on your headstone, pal."

"One minute, why don't you clear the room, give me some space," the second man said.

"What happened to the explosion outside we were waiting for?"

"I don't know, do I?" said Larson. "But Stimson said go, so just bloody go."

"Move out the way, I can't see anything in here."

Harvey removed his belt, and quietly fastened it around the two door handles so it couldn't be opened from the inside.

"I'm not leaving you alone, Johnson, you don't exactly have a great track record do you?"

"You hired me to do a job, Lucas."

"So shut up and do it."

"How good are you at running?"

"Why?"

"Because in twenty seconds this vault door's coming off, and I have no idea how big the bang will be."

"I thought you'd done it before?" Larson's voice was anxious.

"I have, well, I've seen it done, but we didn't use as much as this."

"What?"

"Ten seconds, run."

Harvey heard banging on the doors. "It's locked. Let us out. Help!"

Harvey took a slow walk back to the staircase, casually checked up the stairs and walked up to the dark first floor. He ignored the screaming and banging and waited for the blast with his ears and eyes covered.

The explosion was deafening inside the tiled space. It came with a wave of power that seemed to rock the building. A cloud of dust found its way up the stairs, and Harvey saw the yellow lights had been blown out. It was pitch dark. The noise had been deafening, a jumble of audible carnage. Harvey pulled his shirt up to his mouth and walked back down the steps.

The air was black, dust and grit stuck to his watering eyes, and the smell of concrete and lime was heavy in the air.

He stepped off the stairs, and his foot found a large piece of broken concrete in the darkness. Harvey pulled a phone out his pocket to give him some idea of where he was treading. He cursed himself; he normally carried a Maglite in his pocket, a small two-cell torch that had been more than useful on several occasions. But it had been lost, maybe in the taxi crash, he didn't know.

Slowly working his way along the short corridor, he stepped over the broken double doors and around the concrete blocks that had formed the wall. He drew closer to the vault. The huge, thick steel door had been ripped from the vault by the hinges, but the lock still clung to its counter-part, so the door itself leaned up against the entrance.

Harvey saw a leg on the floor beside the vault. He knew the room must be covered in body parts, but there was no need to look. He'd seen dismembered bodies before and it wasn't pretty. He shone the phone into the vault.

The space was ten feet by eight feet inside, Harvey guessed. On one side were shelves, which were only hanging by the fixings on the far end. The ends of the shelves closest to the door now sat on the floor among scattered paperwork. On the left-hand side was a rack that held paintings. A felt base formed the plinth for the large frames. Dividers kept the paintings from touching and held them upright. There were only four paintings, each one was covered in a shiny purple cloth. Harvey had expected see more of a haul, but he guessed the reality was that vaults in auction houses didn't store valuables for long, the idea was to move them on.

There was a small wooden box on the floor below the broken shelves, partly hidden by the fallen shelves. It was ten inches square and beautifully finished. A layer of dust had already begun to settle on its surface.

Harvey bent, picked the box up and felt the weight. He guessed at three or four kilos, not heavy, but solid. He opened the two small brass catches on the front and lifted the lid. The box was lined with a soft cushioning and a small square of fine green silk lay over the centre.

Harvey lifted the corner of the material and exposed the perfectly smooth, ancient, green-stone artefact underneath. The two-century-old, little, fat buddha laid cross-legged in the box and stared up at Harvey. It was only six inches tall and perhaps four inches across the belly.

Harvey looked around the vault, then made his exit. Outside would be crawling with police by now. He stopped at the bottom of the stairs and considered his options. He was

wanted for murder, a car with his prints on had been suspi-
ciously abandoned outside, and now he was walking into the
street, where the police would be looking for him, with an
ancient priceless buddha.

He took one step onto the stairs.

"It's a dilemma isn't it, Mr Stone?" said a woman's voice. It
was the voice of a confident woman who was used to having
her own way.

"Not really."

"You can't walk out of here with that," she said.

Harvey searched the darkness above him for the source of
the voice.

"Why don't you let me take it off you?" she said. "You
might get away, you might not. I just hope the police don't
shoot you on sight before they know you're one of them."

Harvey didn't reply. Patience.

"You should respect your betters, Harvey, I thought John
would have taught you that."

"He taught me you need to earn respect."

"And haven't I earned it?"

"I don't know. Why don't you tell me?"

"Ah come on, Harvey, we both know where the brains lie."

The woman stepped into the light from the ground floor
above and looked down at Harvey. It was the woman from
the manor house.

"Bring me the buddha, Harvey. This'll be over soon, and
you can go back to playing cops and robbers."

"I think we're playing a pretty good game of it
right now."

"I'm not your average robber, Harvey."

"I'm not your average cop."

"You're not the average anything, are you?"

Harvey didn't reply. Her voice was mature yet had a
youthful element of fun. She was well spoken, like she was

used to being around wealthy individuals, but hadn't been born into wealth.

"I've always wanted to chat with you. I always thought it would be nice to sit and talk one day, Harvey, you know? Really talk."

"I'm not really the talkative type."

"And that's what makes you intriguing. A man like you could do well with a girl like me."

"I've managed pretty well without you so far."

"Join me, Harvey. Don't you miss it? The chase? This thrill of the hunt?"

"I never stopped hunting."

"But you feed someone else now."

"I feed myself."

"But where's the next meal coming from?"

Harvey didn't reply. The woman stepped down onto the first step.

"There you are," she said, "in all your glory. I've watched you for years, you know? Admired you."

"I would have remembered you."

"Oh, you remember me, Harvey. I'm the one that was always one step ahead of you."

"Nobody springs to mind."

"I have friends too, friends that may be of interest to you."

Harvey didn't reply.

"Come closer."

Harvey walked slowly up the stairs to the first floor then stood still.

"That's it. Such a powerful man. Tell me how it felt."

"How what felt?"

"Oh, so many things, Harvey, where to start? Tell me about our mutual friend, Thomson."

"Terry Thomson?"

"Yes, Terence, not his spoiled little whining son. Terry was a king, how did it feel to destroy him?"

Harvey didn't reply.

"Did you feel his power?"

"Not really."

"No? That surprises me, Harvey. Did he fight?"

"No, he opened his arms to it."

"He didn't cry or beg?"

"One of the few that didn't."

"I hear respect."

"No, you don't. He was in the way. He needed stopping."

"I'm glad you did, stop him, that is. He was messing up my plans, he was always interfering."

She knew him. Harvey's memory for faces was good, but he couldn't place her past the manor house.

"And Sergio? That was messy, Harvey, even by your standards."

Harvey didn't reply.

"Are you at peace now, Harvey? I hear Mr Sayan filled in a few blanks for you. Was it the answers you've been searching for, Harvey?"

Harvey didn't reply.

"You must be disappointed in your friend. Do you feel betrayed?"

"I don't feel anything–"

"He taught you well then, Julios I mean."

Harvey didn't reply, but he could hear his own breathing loud against the solid tiled walls.

"Tell me how you feel now, Harvey. How do you remember Julios? As the man that carved you from an angry, broken little boy to the masterpiece you are now? Or do you remember him as the traitor that lied to you your entire life?"

Harvey didn't reply, he wouldn't be pulled down, not now.

"Was anything ever true? I can't imagine how you must feel. So much doubt."

"It won't work, Stimson."

"Ah, clever boy. You've put two and two together."

"That's why nobody ever found you, isn't it, all these years. They searched for a man, a man that never existed."

"Clever boy, I'm surprised nobody else ever figured it out, to be honest. It's not like I ever burst into an armoured van and stole cash or a bank."

"Diamonds," said Harvey. "Always diamonds and jewels."

"And anything that glitters. So pretty." She said the last words with a girly tone.

"And you never killed anyone, impressive."

"No need for that, Harvey, not if you do the job right."

"I thought this place was a little low on security."

"They're all locked away in a storeroom, alive for now, someone will find them when we're gone. No harm done."

"So why the bombs?"

The woman's face sank and her smiled dropped to an emotionless blank expression.

"Not my doing, Harvey, you know me, I'd never-"

"No, you wouldn't. It's okay, you don't have to convince me."

Stimson didn't reply.

"It's your daughter, isn't it?"

Stimson's head jerked up to Harvey.

"The buddha was never for you, it was for Al Sayan, to get your daughter back."

"It was the only way he could get it," she snapped.

"And if somebody wants something priceless, there's only one person to call, right?"

"I refused at first."

"But he took Angel, didn't he? And he took Hague's kid, a bloke like that would never convert, am I right?"

"Help me, Harvey."

"That's strong, all things considered."

"He has more, explosives, I mean."

"The warehouse is empty."

"Don't be a fool, Harvey, you saw the box."

"The box?"

"The wooden crate. You don't need to read German to know what it said, do you?"

Harvey didn't reply.

"How many plastic explosives do you think he had in each of those taxis?"

"He told me there was twenty-five kilos in the one I was in."

"And how much did the box say?"

"A hundred."

"Plus, of course, he has a small army of devout men, all just *dying* to help."

"Not funny."

"I'm sorry, poor Denver. That was unnecessary."

"Tell me what the plan was."

"The exchange?"

Harvey didn't reply.

"We meet, I give him the buddha, I get Angel back."

"She's a sweet girl."

"You saw her?"

"We shared the same accommodation."

"The warehouse?"

"She's safe."

"Safe? None of us are safe if Al Sayan *does* get the buddha."

"So let's get him first."

"I want to see Angel."

"Take me to Al Sayan."

"Angel first."

"Then what?" asked Harvey.

"You give me the buddha, and I take it to Al Sayan."

"In return for what? He doesn't have Angel anymore."

"He doesn't want Angel, he wants the buddha." She sighed loud in the stairwell. "He says it'll fund his campaign to cleanse Britain."

"What's to stop me walking out of here and handing you over?"

"You won't get Al Sayan, and he'll bomb the crap out of whatever he needs to get what he wants. Could you live with that? Knowing you had the chance to save lives?"

"You want to see Angel?"

"Or you don't get Al Sayan."

"She's close."

"So show me, I need to see her." It wasn't the demand of a scheming criminal mastermind on the brink of walking off with a priceless antique, it was the plea of a broken-hearted mother who'd had her daughter kidnapped by terrorists.

The door behind Stimson opened, and light flooded the dim corridor where she stood.

"Mummy?"

"Angel?"

"Don't move, Stimson." Melody walked through the door carrying the girl. The girl reached her hand out towards her mother. Stimson took a step towards her, but Melody moved back to the doorway. "I told you not to move."

"Mummy."

"It's okay, darling, Mummy's here. Are you okay? Are you hurt?"

The girl shook her head.

"Are you hurt? Has anybody hurt you?"

The girl shook her head,

"You've seen her, now take us to Al Sayan," said Harvey.

"Honey, mummy has to go somewhere, but this lady will look after you, just for a little while longer."

Harvey took a step up the stairs towards Stimson as her back was turned to Melody and the child. He felt the nuzzle of a gun in his back and closed his eyes.

"She'll be safe with me," said Melody. "Harvey let's go."

"I seem to have met your friend, Stimson."

"Ah yes, my private security." She looked over his shoulder at the man standing behind Harvey.

"You going to call him off?"

"I need *some* security, Harvey, I'm sure you can empathise."

"Tell him to drop the gun."

"No idle threats, Harvey."

"I don't make threats."

"He's good you know, one of the best bodyguards a girl can have."

"I'm sure he is. Call him off. We have Angel."

"Security is his blood, you know?"

"Great, call him off."

"I think you two will get along."

"Not with a gun in my back we won't."

"True. Adeo."

Harvey felt the dull point of the gun being removed from his back.

"Adeo?" asked Harvey.

"That's right, Harvey, Adeo."

"I told you it's in his blood, he comes from a long line of highly dangerous men."

Adeo gave a deep and short laugh behind him. It had the depth of a man with a broad chest, a large neck and wide shoulders. It was a laugh much like Julios'. In fact, it was nearly exactly the same.

"You can catch up later, I'm sure you have a lot to talk about," said Stimson. "Let's go."

Melody disappeared from sight back outside. "All clear," she said over the comms.

Harvey walked up the stairs. Once again, his mind rallied through his memories of Julios, who'd told Harvey his brother was dead. This time, Harvey channelled his anger. He let it flow through him, feed his tired muscles, and feed his hunger for Al Sayan.

He stepped outside into the bright daylight, still carrying the box.

The Volvo was parked outside behind the van Larson had used. The van's hazard lights still blinked. Reg sat in the driver's seat with Frank beside him. Melody had climbed in the back and was pulling the seat belt across Angel.

Harvey walked up the few steps to the pavement and stood beside the car. He turned and watched Adeo come up the steps, his huge legs hauling his massive weight. Harvey studied his face; he was, without question, related to Julios. It was like an old memory, like thinking of a face you used to know, but you can't quite place the features correctly.

Adeo had Julios' nose, his family nose, and his jawline was wide and strong like his brother's had been. But Adeo's brow was deeper, which gave him a dumb look. He was also bigger than Julios had been. Harvey remembered Julios telling him that he was the eldest of the two, and had cared for his younger sibling, as Hannah had cared for Harvey.

"Fond memories, Harvey?" said Stimson.

"Ancient history."

"Talking of ancient history," she gestured to the box.

"What's the plan?"

"I call him, he tells us where to meet."

"Then what?" asked Harvey.

"You give me the buddha, I go meet him."

"And?"

"He shows himself, you take him out, Mills here gives me my daughter back."

"Somebody needs to go to prison here," said Frank. He'd climbed out of the car and stood leaning on the Audi's roof. "You know the score, Stimson."

"I don't see why it needs to get nasty, Franky."

Frank stared at her shaking his head.

"What?" said Stimson, "Surprised you've been outwitted by a woman all these years?"

Harvey stared at her too. She was worthy of a stare. She obviously looked after herself. Harvey judged her as early thirties, his age, but knew better. She'd been on the scene since he was young, he'd heard the stories.

Beneath her long fur coat, she wore a tight red dress and matching heels. She was strikingly beautiful with a figure that most men would fall for.

"It's rude to stare, Harvey. Didn't Julios teach you that?" said Stimson, turning to Harvey.

Adeo grinned.

"Your time's up, Stimson. When this is over, you'll be taking a holiday," said Frank.

"That's right, I need a break, some time with my daughter perhaps."

"Her Majesty's pleasure, Stimson."

"Oh, Franky."

"Work with us, and I'll see all things are considered."

"All things are considered? What things, Frank?"

"The robbery for a start?"

"Wasn't me."

"Larson?"

"Larson who?"

"Lucas Larson, your number one."

"I don't know what you're talking about. I've never seen or spoken to anyone named Larson, have I, Adeo?"

The big man shook his head and jutted his lower lip out in denial.

"You have nothing on me, Carver."

"People have died, you callous bitch."

"I don't think there's much need for that kind of language in front of my daughter if you wouldn't mind."

"You can't get away with this," said Frank.

"I take you to Al Sayan, you let me go."

"You take us to Al Sayan, you get your daughter back, that was the deal."

A mobile phone began to ring. The noise came from Stimson's clutch.

"Mind if I get this? It's kind of life and death."

She pulled the sleek looking smartphone from her bag, tapped the screen with a perfectly manicured nail and held the phone to her ear. Harvey saw the glistening earring beside the phone and the sparkling ring on her finger. He followed the contours of her body and saw the bright watch on her slender arm beneath the fur sleeve.

She pulled the phone from her ear, disconnected the call and put it back in her bag. She snapped the clutch shut with finality.

"Tower Bridge, one hour."

22

LOVE THY BEAST

MELODY, FRANK AND REG TRAVELLED IN THE VOLVO, while Harvey and Stimson rode in the little Porsche. The buddha rode in the Porsche's small rear seat, and Adeo followed in the van.

"He wants me alone," said Stimson.

"I'm sure he's not the only man out there that wants you alone, Stimson."

"I'm sure." She smiled, pleased at his recognition of her looks.

"I'm sure there's a few men out there ready to choke the life out of you," said Harvey. He didn't face her, he carried on looking out the window. He felt her smile fade.

"Any police on the scene and he hits the bang button," she said.

"Any idea where he's planted it?"

"He didn't say."

"Taxis?"

"He didn't say."

"So it could be nothing? He might not have anything."

"Bit of risk though, Harvey, isn't it?"

"Frank's got the river police standing by, and there'll be armed police all over."

"What Al Sayan doesn't know shouldn't hurt him," said Stimson.

"Oh it'll hurt alright, but it won't be the police that hurts him."

Stimson looked across at Harvey. "You're not going to hand him over are you?"

"He's got a debt to pay," said Harvey.

There was a silence.

"And me?" said Stimson.

"What about you?"

"Haven't I a debt to pay?"

"Not really. It's a transaction. You give me Al Sayan, and you get your daughter back. As you said, Frank probably doesn't have anything on you anyway."

"So he'll stand by his word, will he?"

"Most honest man I know."

"That doesn't say much, you grew up with villains."

"Pot, kettle," said Harvey.

"Pot, kettle," agreed Stimson.

"Ever wished you did something else?" asked Harvey.

"Like ordinary people?" replied Stimson. "No, I wasn't made for that life." Stimson checked her rearview mirror.

"She's still there," said Harvey. "You can trust Melody."

"She's cute."

Harvey didn't reply. Melody overtook them on Upper Thames Street and sped off to get in position.

"Some might say," replied Harvey.

"Have I come between y-"

"You've come between nothing, Stimson," snapped Harvey. "What you have stepped into though is a team of very angry people who just lost their friend because of you. And I'll be honest, I don't know how long I can keep this friendly charade up for. It's your fault we're in this, and I'm doing my very best not to lean across this car and rip your throat out."

"I had to."

"Had to what?"

"Bring you into it," replied Stimson. "You would have got wind of it anyway, you were *supposed* to fall for the decoy."

"The manor house?"

"Yes, you should have been concentrating all your efforts into understanding how on earth anyone could carry out a heist in such a place."

"That's ridiculous, I took one look and knew it was impossible."

"Ah, but impossible is my speciality, right?"

"You go for the hard to get, I'll give you that."

"Is that what you are, Harvey? Hard to get?"

Harvey didn't reply.

"If you'd have just stayed out in Essex, you'd have been fine," said Stimson.

"You dumped a body in my house."

"Al Sayan did. Killing's not my style remember?"

"Right."

"What about the fake cop?"

"Ah, that was me."

"Not very well planned, I saw through it. Plus we got you on the dash cam."

"It was last minute, you shouldn't have followed us."

"In fact, I've seen through all your plans and schemes."

"It's not been my finest hour, Harvey, I'll admit that, but the stakes were high."

"Angel."

Stimson nodded.

"You need to disappear after this."

"I know, I've made the arrangements."

"Where?"

Stimson raised her eyebrows.

"Worth a try," said Harvey.

"Join me?"

It was Harvey's turn to give Stimson a look.

"Worth a try. I bet a man like you could take care of a girl like me. There must be a lot of women out there that sat and stared at you wondering what you'd be like. Wondered how it would feel to have a beast on top of them, what it would be like dancing with the devil. A moment of taboo ecstasy perhaps?" She paused. "How about it?"

"I'm not for hire."

"I wouldn't be paying, not cash anyway."

Harvey heard a click on his ear-piece. "Mills in place."

"ETA one minute," replied Harvey.

"Is that her?" Stimson asked. "She's a lucky girl."

"I'm not her type."

"But she's yours?"

"Talk me through the plan."

I stop the car here." She pulled over in St Katherine's Way, which was on the north side of Tower Bridge and on the opposite side of the road to the Tower of London. "I climb up those steps, walk to the middle of the bridge and give Al Sayan the buddha."

"Then?"

"Then I come back, and your sweetheart gives me my daughter back."

"And Al Sayan?"

"Not my problem."

"Al Sayan is in position," said Melody. "I have him in my sight."

Harvey looked away from Stimson. "Sit tight Melody. He's placed something somewhere."

"Say again?"

"There's one more package. His fall back plan."

"But there were only three taxis?"

"I'm thinking the meeting on the bridge isn't just a convenient location."

"Say hello from me, won't you?" said Stimson.

"Save the girly chat for when you see her and tell her yourself," said Harvey, getting out of the car. "Grab the buddha and let's go."

"You're going *with* me?"

"You don't think I'm going to stand and watch you walk away with that thing do you?" Harvey strode towards the stairs up to the bridge. Stimson locked the car and chased after him.

"He'll blow it up, all the people."

"*Harvey, are you sure about this?*" said Melody over the comms.

"What people?" Harvey turned and squared up to her. "So far it's all been about you, hasn't it? And if it hasn't been about you, it's been about your daughter or you not going to prison, or you trying to break me down. You just lost Lucas Larson, a taxi driver lost his life, and God knows about the other two and what about all those people in Canary Wharf? And what about-"

"Denver?" said Stimson. "Is that it? You finally lost someone too, so now you're mad. Well, good. That's what we need, that's what this *city* needs right now is for Harvey Stone to get mad and stop Al Sayan."

"So tell me where his next target is, tell me where I need to be."

"You need to be up there with me, you need to chuck the lunatic off the bridge."

"Is that what you want or is that what he wants?" said Harvey. Stimson closed her mouth. "That's it, isn't it? He wants me, and you're going to let him take me."

Stimson didn't reply.

"And with me out of the way, you can go back to being the spoiled little bitch who gets all the diamonds."

"I don't want all the diamonds." Stimson pulled a ring off her finger and threw it at Harvey. "I just want my daughter." She stood in front of Harvey looking helpless, dejected and broken.

"Let's go."

Stimson didn't move, she just stood there in the road.

"Don't give me that, pick up your ring up and get up those stairs. If you were upset, you'd have been upset before I told you she was safe."

Harvey climbed to the top of the stairs, stood on the bridge and looked along it. The shape and length of the bridge meant he couldn't see to the middle from where he stood. But he could see where Melody said she'd be, on the top section intended for maintenance. If Melody said Al Sayan was there already, then he was there.

He began to walk. Stimson had slipped off her heels and ran to catch Harvey up.

"Give me the buddha."

"No, I need to-"

"Give me the buddha, Stimson." He held out his hand.

"Wow, I like it when you're angry." She passed him the buddha. She had removed it from the box and its covering. Harvey felt it. It felt like any old ornament you might find in any old house. It was just sickly green.

"I'm not angry," said Harvey.

"What are you then? Moody, quiet, sultry?"

"I'm focused. I'm taking this bastard down, and you're a distraction. Or is that your game too? Distract me so he can kill me?"

Stimson didn't reply.

"You're smart, I know you're smart. You don't have to

prove it, I'm smart too." He gestured with the buddha. "Walk in front and walk fast."

Harvey saw Al Sayan from a hundred yards away and checked his comms were open. The Arab was unmistakable in Harvey's mind now. As Harvey walked forwards, he saw a large bag by Al Sayan's feet. Harvey hid nothing, not even with the rage that was boiling inside of him, feeding him.

"Mr Harvey, thank you for joining us."

"Let's make this short, shall we?" said Harvey.

"That's fine by me, I see you've brought me a gift, how kind."

"Stimson is blocking my view," said Melody.

"Don't get too close to him, Stimson," said Harvey.

"I'm not wearing my vest," said Al Sayan. He looked down to the bag by his feet.

"Where's the explosives?"

Stimson moved back away from him and stood beside Harvey.

"If I tell you that, I lose my upper hand." Al Sayan smiled. "Can't we just carry out the transaction without the need for all the games and power play?"

Harvey didn't reply.

"I didn't think so" Al Sayan continued. "I know you took the brat, the offspring of this tart. So I took my own precautions. If you give me the buddha, and I walk away, who's to say your other little slut friend won't shoot me in the back?"

Harvey didn't reply.

"That's what I thought, Mr Harvey," said Al Sayan. "That's why you're going wear this vest until I'm safely out of the way. I'll call Stimson's phone when you can take it off, and we can all go on with our lives."

"As long as you're here in this country, you won't be safe."

"I'll take my chances, Mr Harvey," said Al Sayan. "Put the vest on." He slid the bag across to Harvey with his foot.

You win some, you lose some, Mr Harvey. Isn't that what you say?"

"And what is it you say?"

"I don't, I just win. Put it on."

Harvey picked up the bag off the floor carefully and unzipped it.

"It's quite safe to handle."

Harvey saw the police boat in the water below him. It had stopped other smaller vessels from passing under the bridge, Frank had obviously made some calls. The police boat was small, and an officer stood on the rear deck waving his hands to the other larger boats, which were mostly tourist vessels. Groups of people stood on the decks and happily snapped away at the attraction, oblivious to the danger as Harvey donned the vest.

"Zip it up. It's quite snug," said Al Sayan. "It's my own work."

Harvey didn't reply. He slid the zipper up to his chest. Stimson looked on at him wide-eyed.

"What the hell are you doing, Harvey?" said Melody over the comms.

Harvey stared at Stimson. "This is what you wanted, wasn't it?"

"No, it's not."

"Stimson leaves now," said Harvey.

"I don't think so," replied AL Sayan.

"Where's the detonator?"

"Hidden. Inside the vest. But it's okay, it's fully automatic. All I have to do is call the phone that's connected, and-"

"And?"

"It'll all be over," said Al Sayan.

"I'll find you."

"Maybe, maybe not," replied Al Sayan. "Now pass me my prize."

Harvey stopped. He controlled his breathing but could feel his heart racing.

He held his hand out in front of him. The jade buddha stared back at him.

"Put it on the floor, Mr Harvey. I don't trust you."

Harvey swung his hand out to his left and held the buddha over the water.

"Ball's in your court, Al Sayan," said Harvey. "Tell your man to back down."

"Harvey no, stop," cried Melody over the comms. Harvey heard the tone of her voice, she was ready to break.

"Is this what you call a stalemate?" asked Al Sayan.

"No, it's what I call you telling your man to back down."

Al Sayan held his phone up. "If I dial this number, we all die."

"That solves the problem then, doesn't it?"

"Harvey, no," Stimson pleaded. "Just give him the buddha."

"You should listen to her, she's wise."

"She's smart, not wise. If she was wise, we wouldn't be standing here."

"If you drop the buddha, more people die," said Al Sayan coldly.

"If I drop the buddha, you die."

"And then the people die."

"I guess you could call them martyrs then, because if you die too, how many more lives will be saved?"

"I'm tired of these games, Mr Harvey." Al Sayan's voice grew harsher. "Put the buddha on the floor, or the people die."

Harvey didn't reply.

"Please, Harvey, don't do this," said Melody.

"Why do you want this so badly? You don't look like a collector."

"What does a collector look like? Or another way of looking at it, Mr Harvey, could be what is it I'm collecting?"

"You're not collecting anything, you're just brainwashed."

"Easy now, no need for insults."

"I don't get it, you people, you're all mouth when it comes to the spineless act of blowing up innocent people, but a little banter, and you get all upset."

"Mr Harvey, that will not do-"

"Don't tell me what I can and can't say. Listen to yourself. You're weak, hiding behind a bag of explosives because you don't have the intelligence to fight a war like the rest of civilisation."

"Don't have the intelligence?" shouted Al Sayan. "Who do you think orchestrated this little saga? It wasn't me that robbed the auction house, was it? No, Mr Harvey, it was you that walked out with the buddha. And who was it that dragged this whore out of her cave? How long had you been looking for her? Years, Mr Harvey, years. And you have the gall to mock my intelligence. Put the vest on, stop this nonsense."

"You put the phone down, I'll put the buddha down, and we'll fight like men. How does that sound?"

"Have you any idea what that is worth?"

"Nothing to me."

"What you have in your hands, Mr Harvey, will fuel my plans to cleanse this wretched country for as long as it takes. The war on the west will never stop until all the infidels are wiped off the face of the planet. And only those who believe in the one true God, and worship him as the prophet Mohammed said we should, are free to walk the streets. Without fear, without pain, without suffering. With food in their bellies and roofs over their heads and future. Mr Harvey, don't you see? To change the west and to spread the will of the one true God will take more than a few small explosions.

This is only the awakening, my friend. This is the birth of
Islam and the downfall of Christianity, a religion that has
mocked the rest of the world for far too long. When the
people of London are untied with Allah, the rest of the
country shall fall. And when England falls, the rest of the
western world will tumble down around it."

"You make me sick."

"You will be one of the first, Mr Harvey, to fall in the
name of Islam, but nobody will remember your name.
Nobody will sing for the fallen hero. But they will remember
me. They will remember my face as I stand upon the ashes of
Christianity and build mosques so that the beloved can pray.
It will be me that is remembered five hundred years from
now, Mr Harvey."

"And this little statue will do all that, will it?"

"No, Mr Harvey, but that little statue, as you call it, will
fund my campaign to free the west. When London falls, I will
have all the riches I need." Al Sayan stopped and eyed Harvey.
"How easy it would be to purchase a few passenger jets. How
easy it would be to bring the once great empire of Britain to
its knees. That, Mr Harvey, in your hand, is the key to the
future of England."

"You won't make it off this bridge."

"Try me," said Al Sayan. He lifted his phone. "I'm growing
tired of this, I'm afraid I really just make a call."

"I don't care what you do," said Harvey. Blow me up, blow
the bridge up, but there's no way I'm handing this over to you
until you tell your man to stand down.

"You don't follow the rules, do you?"

Harvey didn't reply.

"Okay, okay. I will tell my man to stand down," said Al
Sayan. "But you pass the buddha to Stimson first. She can act
as escrow."

Harvey slowly brought the buddha back. He stared hard at Stimson, gauging her allegiance.

"Do it, Mr Harvey."

Harvey handed Stimson the jade buddha.

"Call him off. Now."

"Easily done," said Al Sayan. He turned away and looked down to the group of boats. Tourists huddled on the decks staring up at the scene that played out in front of them. Al Sayan nodded and the driver of one boat put the engines in reverse and began to move away from the pack, away from the kill zone.

"Oh my God, it's one of the boats. I have him. I have the driver in my sights," said Melody. "What do you want to do?"

Harvey watched Al Sayan's man from the bridge. The hate was brimming inside him. Over a hundred people were stood on the boats below, they'd all be torn to shreds and drowned.

"Now," said Harvey.

The shot fired before he'd finished saying the one-syllable word. The small glass window of the boat's cabin smashed and the rest of the glass was spattered with the driver's blood. He slumped to the floor and out of sight. Women screamed far below, and the police boat jumped into action. Its bow raised up as soon as the driver slammed the throttles forward.

"You just lost your bargaining power," said Harvey and stepped forward toward Al Sayan. He reached out and grabbed his neck with one hand and smashed the heel of his hand into the man's face.

"Go, go, go," Melody called over the comms, and the sound of sirens filled the air.

Harvey dragged Al Sayan to his feet. Blood ran down the Afghan's face and clumped in his long, straggly beard. He smiled up at Harvey and hit the green *Call* button on the cheap Nokia.

———

Melody sprinted up the stairs of the bridge. The space was empty; tourists had been told to leave when Frank had called it into his superiors, and the message had filtered down to the bridge's tourist operators.

Melody reached the top of the north tower. The glass floor gave her a great view down between the bridge's structures but didn't afford her the shot she needed. She pulled the Diemaco's strap over her head and climbed off the viewing platform onto the old stone walls at the top of the tower. Melody worked her way around until she had a clear view of Al Sayan, stood alone in the centre of the bridge.

"Mills in position," she said over the comms. She didn't need any reply. The plan didn't stretch any further than Melody going up and taking Al Sayan out. Then Harvey told her about the fall back bomb. That changed the outcome. She could take Al Sayan out anytime, but innocent people would die.

Patience. She thought of Harvey's mantra. Patience, planning and execution. She could be as patient as she liked, but the planning was out the window. There were too many variables. She made herself comfortable. The rifle's bipod stood on the parapet like an archer of days gone by. She held Al Sayan in her sight.

Boats passed under the bridge, tourists off to see the Tower of London's famous Traitors' Gate, where doomed convicts would be taken in from the river, unlikely to ever see the sky again. The Tower of London's history is full of stories of death and suffering, Medieval London, rats and executioners. Whatever happened in the next hour would determine if that storybook had another tale of death added to its collection.

She noted the flags on the Tower's tall flagpoles. The

wind was a constant south-easterly, five to six knots. Melody adjusted the scope accordingly, moving only four clicks to account for the difference in height between Al Sayan and the flags.

She heard Harvey had switched the comms to open and Melody had heard their conversation?. The conversation between him and Stimson had been personal. They were like old friends that had never met. Stimson was cunning, but her allegiance was clear. She would be loyal to no-one but herself.

Harvey was going onto the bridge with Stimson. That changed things. He was putting lives at risk.

"Harvey are you sure about this?"

He gave no reply to Melody, but she heard the argument between him and Stimson, and could do nothing about it from where she was sat.

Melody watched the two of them walk across the bridge towards Al Sayan. She watched how Harvey controlled her, and how Stimson let him. Stimson had made several comments about Harvey and Melody, including enough questions that Melody had asked herself. What would Harvey be like? But the answers were always the same. He would be selfish, cold and mean. She'd grown to love the man, he was lovable, but in the same way she loved Reg, and had loved Denver. They'd shared close calls and boring nights of surveillance in the back of the van, but that was it. It was platonic. She loved Harvey enough to be worried about him. So when she saw him put the explosive vest on, her heart began to race. Al Sayan moved up and down in her sight. She fought to control her breathing but struggled; Harvey was killing himself.

"What the hell are you doing, Harvey?"

He held the buddha over the water.

Al Sayan remained composed. He had nothing to lose.

What can you take from a man who is ready to die for his cause? The ultimate sacrifice.

"Harvey, no, stop," she cried.

But Harvey didn't reply. He continued to hold his hand out over the water.

Melody tried to regain her own composure. Al Sayan still stood in her sight, but tears clouded Melody's vision. She wiped them away, but her sight was still blurred. She felt the tears run down her own cheeks.

"Please, Harvey, don't do this."

Harvey passed the buddha to Stimson. Melody wiped her eyes and refocused. She found Al Sayan. He turned away and gave a signal to somebody below. Melody tracked along and the driver who had begun to reverse a boat full of tourists.

"I have the driver in my sights. What do you want to do?"

"Now," said Harvey. His voice was calm, clear and crisp over the ear-piece. And Melody squeezed the trigger the final eighth of an inch.

She immediately brought the rifle back to Al Sayan and saw Harvey reach for him. Harvey delivered a blow and dragged the man to his feet, but then there was a pause. Silence. It was like time stood still for a second, maybe two.

Then Harvey wrenched the man close to him and launched them both over the wall, down and out of sight.

"No," Melody screamed. She dropped the rifle and ran to the far side of the parapet but could see nothing. Tourists peered overboard searching the water with camera phones, ready to capture an explosion, so the police ordered the boat drivers to disperse with frantic waving of their arms. The Thames is tidal, and the river was flowing out to sea, but its strong currents beneath the surface were violent and unpredictable. More police boats standing by joined in the search and the comms was a riot of noise as Frank and Reg began to call to each other.

A few seconds passed, then a muffled explosion shook the water beneath the bridge. A circle of power ran out from the quietened blast in a violent shock wave. It then dispersed, and the river resumed its flow.

Melody sank to the floor and dropped her head. This time she let the tears flow, and released her grip on the bursts of emotion that came from inside her in uncontrollable sobs. She did love him, she had loved him. She wanted to tell him. She wanted to go back to when they had stood on the riverside outside headquarters. Turn back even further to when he had pulled her from the sea and saved her life. She wanted to see him smile, make him smile and smile with him.

She climbed down unsteadily from the top of the tower onto the viewing platform, and fell the last few feet to the floor. Her vision was foggy and her head was dizzy. Pulling herself up, she leaned on the wall for stability. Slowly, she made her way to the stairs and walked down.

Reg was stood in the ancient doorway, silhouetted by the bright light outside. She knew it was Reg by his shape, his posture. He held his arms out, and she fell into him. Reg held her tight, and her tears returned. Her body convulsed as the sobs came.

"Let it out, it's okay, let it out." Reg stroked her hair.

"It's over, Reg," she said into his shoulder. "We can't go on, not now."

Melody pulled the ear-piece form her ear and threw it on the floor. She stepped away from Reg and stamped on the device, crushing it beneath her foot.

"Take a breath, Melody," said Reg in a surprisingly soft tone.

"I'm sorry," said Melody, wiping her eyes and trying hard to focus. "Where's Stimson?"

"Disappeared," he said. "She was there when..." Reg paused. "When he went over, and then she'd gone. The big guy was sitting with the girl the whole time, but by the time we realised Stimson had gone, we saw that he'd gone too, and the girl. We were distracted."

"So we lost?" asked Melody. Her mouth hung open in exhausted exasperation.

"He didn't die in vain, Melody. He took down Al Sayan."

"But we lost Stimson and the buddha," said Melody. "And we lost Harvey."

"There's nothing I can say to bring him back, Melody. But what would Harvey do now?"

"He'd kick ass," said Melody between sobs.

"So let's go kick ass."

"How? What with?" said Melody. She broke away from Reg. "We don't have anything, no suspects, no tech, no nothing." She sounded dejected and looked defeated.

"Don't do this, Melody," replied Reg. "Don't let Harvey's death be the end of you. Don't let it be for nothing."

Melody didn't reply.

"Let's go," he said, "for Harvey."

"And Denver," said Melody.

"For both of them," said Reg.

23

DOWN WITH THE SERPENT

MELODY AND REG WALKED TO THE WAITING AUDI. "MIND if I drive, sir?" She opened the boot and placed the Diemaco carefully inside.

Frank got out the car and walked to the passenger side. Reg climbed into the back seat and pulled his belt on.

"You ready, Reg?" she asked, then gunned the accelerator without waiting for his response.

"Can you get access to LUCY, Reg?"

"Of course I can," replied Reg. "Easy girl," he added as the large saloon car slid into the outside lane.

"No time for easy, Reg. If they reach a plane, that's it, game over," replied Melody. The Audi's engine roared out of a bend in the road using both lanes. Melody felt the car control the slide and shift the power to the inside wheels.

"Okay, I'm inside his profile. I just need to connect to LUCY, and I can pull up the big guy's phone signal, assuming he hasn't lobbed it somewhere."

"Forget the phone, Reg," said Melody, easing the car toward Rotherhithe Tunnel. "Find my jacket."

"Your what?"

"I dropped the tracker from my jacket in Angel's pocket."

"You're a smart girl, Melody," said Frank. "I'll give you that."

"Okay, they're currently on the A12 heading out of town."

Melody swerved around a slow driver in the fast lane of the tunnel approach road, then dropped down a gear. "Hold on."

The noise of the car's high-performance engine inside the tunnel was loud enough to alert the drivers in front that a car was coming up fast. Reg looked on in horror as cars strived to reach the inside lane before the Audi reached them. Frank held onto the door handle, but remained silent. Twice Melody had to guide the Audi between a lorry and stubborn driver who refused to move. Reg held his hands up to his face, unable to look at the catastrophe he was sure was about to happen.

When they finally emerged from the tunnel, Melody once again dropped down into third gear and launched though the traffic that fought for the exit lane. The Audi roared past the other cars in a blur. The A12 stretched out in front of them. Miles and miles of multi-lane fast roads led from the city all the way to Ipswich on the East Coast.

"Okay, Reg, find me all the airfields on our path."

"All the airfields?" Reg replied. "That's going to be quite a few."

"Start with the closest one."

"There's a small airfield near Upminster in Essex, not busy and unlicensed. Another in Noak Hill, again not busy, quite small and unlicensed. The main licensed airfield heading east would be Stapleford Abbots."

"Stapleford Abbots?" said Melody. "Why do I know that name?"

"It's about three miles from Theydon Bois," said Frank. "That'll be where she's heading."

"Theydon Bois?" asked Melody.

"John Cartwright's house," replied Frank. "It's where Stone grew up, where Stimson would end all this."

"What makes you think that?"

"You heard them talking, Stimson's playing games with him, she wants him. Wanted him," Frank corrected himself. "She would have had no idea that Harvey wouldn't survive. Imagine it. Harvey learns that Julios wasn't the man he always thought he was. He's devastated, lost faith in everything. Taking him back there invokes memories for him. She offers him work, freedom, answers. You don't think she told him all that crap about his life because she felt like having a chat with another old villain do you?" Frank sighed. "No, she was enticing him. She was telling him how much she knows, about him, about his past, about his life. She was going to try and take him from us. If there's a plane waiting for her, it's there in Stapleford."

"You need a route, Melody?"

"I could drive there with my eyes closed after what happened there." Melody wiped her eyes at the mention of Harvey and concentrated on the road, though her head was bursting.

"Where exactly can she fly to from Stapleford?" asked Reg. "Runway looks pretty short from the satellite."

"It's mainly small aircraft, Cessnas and the such, but even they can make it to France easily without refuelling. From France, she could go anywhere," said Frank.

"What happens if she gets away with the buddha?" asked Melody. "What's the consequence here?"

Frank saw that Melody was stringing out the conversation, avoiding long silences where her mind could wander off to Harvey.

"Failed case? Strike one."

"Even-"

"Even if we have taken Al Sayan down? Yes."

"Where does that leave us?"

"Well we won't be shut down, the case will stay open, but too many fails and the unit will break up. The unit's not official yet anyway, so all they'll do is place you two somewhere else, and I'll take early retirement."

"Was it true what you said about your wife being killed by Al Sayan, sir?" asked Melody.

"I wouldn't lie about something like that, Mills."

"Could have been motivational."

"No, it was true," said Frank. He gave a large exhale. "She was one of the unlucky ones."

"Sorry, sir," said Melody quietly.

"What are you sorry for, Mills?"

"For pushing," she replied. "For your loss."

"It's the world where we live in, isn't it?" said Frank. "It's a cruel, cruel world. We spend most of our days saving up to retire, then when we're finally ready, things have changed so much we don't want to anymore. Not here anyway. There's no freedom and too many memories."

"And if you could change it?" asked Melody.

"I'd take freedom over comfort. Security over choice. And friends over memories, Mills."

Melody heard the words and let them roll around her mind. She looked across at him, and he gave her a smile that said *I know how you're feeling*.

"Okay, I have Melody's jacket turning off the M11 motorway heading toward Stapleford," said Reg from the back.

"We're ten minutes behind them," said Melody. "It's going to take some doing to catch them up once they're on the back roads."

"Open her up, Mills," said Frank.

"Go big or go home, sir?" said Reg.

"Something like that, Tenant."

The team made the turning off the M11 in six minutes. "Stimson is five minutes out from the airfield, we are eleven if we maintain speed," confirmed Reg.

Melody slid the Audi skilfully off the exit ramp and wound the engine back up as fast as the A-road would allow. The smaller roads in the village of Abridge meant the team had to slow for a brief time. But, as soon as they had passed through it, Melody slammed the car into third gear and wound the engine back up.

"Stimson is in the airfield. We can only assume the plane is ready for takeoff, and that she'll park nearby," said Reg.

"How fond of this car are you, sir?" asked Melody.

"Why?" asked Frank.

"They're on the runway, and we're not. I'm just-"

"Airfield entrance is coming in five hundred metres," said Reg.

"Do what you need to do Mills," said Frank.

"Copy that, sir," replied Melody. She touched on the brakes, eased into third and let the gearbox slow them down a fraction. Then, dropping into second, she span the wheel and popped the clutch as the car started to turn out of the bend. The rear end slid nicely out. The front smashed the gates open and tore one of the wing mirrors from its hinges. Melody straightened the car up and found third.

"Reg, be my eyes, there's a hundred planes here," said Melody calmly.

"One o'clock, eight hundred yards," replied Reg without hesitation.

"That's the runway," said Frank.

"I have a visual," said Melody. "They're taxiing for takeoff. Reg, pull the back seat down and grab the Diemaco from the boot. Sir, care for a drive?" Melody didn't wait for an answer.

She hit the cruise control button on the steering wheel and pushed her seat all the way back.

"Mills," said Frank "What are-"

"Left foot first, sir."

Frank moved his left leg over to the driver's side. "For God's sake-"

"You got the wheel?"

"I have it, I don't know what-"

"Okay, all yours sir," said Melody. She hit the button on the rear door and lowered the window. Frank climbed fully into the driver's seat and pulled it forwards. The car veered slightly as he took control, but he brought it back on course.

"Get me alongside them, sir. I'll take the tyres out," shouted Melody over the rushing wind from the open window.

"Let's try this my way first, Mills." Frank gave a dab of brakes to turn off the cruise control, then dropped the car into second and spun onto the runway. The little Cessna was three hundred yards ahead.

"They're leaving," shouted Reg. The little plane sat at the end of the runway and worked up its engine.

"Two hundred yards," called Reg.

The pilot released the brakes, and the Cessna began to accelerate along the tarmac.

"One hundred yards."

"Sir," said Melody, "whats the plan here? I can take the tyres out before they get airborne."

They drew level with the plane and Frank guided the car under its wing and sounded the horn. The pilot refused to heed Frank's call.

Melody ditched the rifle onto Reg, reached out the window to hold the roof bars and pulled herself up to sit on the door.

"Closer," she shouted. Frank eased the Audi in closer until

Melody could reach the wing support, made up of two circular bars connecting the underside to the fuselage. Melody gripped onto the bars and stood on the car door. Her arms were wrapped around the wing support. She pushed off with her feet and swung her legs up over the bars just as the wings began to get lift. The wind against Melody's body froze her hands and threatened to rip her off the wing, but she locked her legs in place and tightened the grip of her left arm. Reaching behind her, she pulled her Sig from her waistband, levelling it at the pilot and gesturing for him to take them back down.

The pilot turned away and spoke to Stimson. Melody saw her gesture for him to continue.

Melody fired two rounds into the fuselage near the back of the plane. The pilot began waving one arm at Stimson, who was leaning forward, telling him to continue.

Stimson stared in disbelief out of the window. Then she turned to the pilot and started shouting. He argued back. Melody could make out the conversation but heard nothing. It was clear he was simply stating that there was a woman on the wing with a gun.

The plane banked sharply, and Melody had to hold on with both arms, but the gun stopped her from gripping the tube. The pilot pulled back on the yoke. Melody was hit by extreme G-force. She fought to hang on, her legs were holding tight, but her gun arm was slipping. Her hands were frozen, and the blast from the propeller deafened her.

Then the pilot eased the plane forward. Melody wasn't ready for the change. She slid around the wing support, reached to grab the other support, and saw her Sig fall to the ground below.

The pilot saw the gun fall and eased the plane back into a steady flight. The little Cessna began to climb.

With the plane stable, Melody was able to adjust her position and began to kick the window of the plane. She tried hard to smash the perspex so she could get inside. She had no doubt that once inside, she could take control.

But before she could settle in for another kick, the door was heaved open. Stimson stood in the doorway, her long coat flapping around and whipping against her body. She looked angry but determined. Holding on with one hand, Stimson reached out to Melody. For a brief moment, Melody thought she was going help her in and was grateful. Then Stimson's hand turned from an open palm to a fierce, well-manicured claw that stabbed into Melody's hands.

Stimson dug in deep and broke skin. Melody gave a yell and gripped with her legs. Her left hand fell from the support, and with each attempt to reach for the tube, the wind and Stimson blocked her. She was forcing Melody off. Her right hand was slipping, she couldn't hold much longer. The wing support was too fat for her hands to grip properly. One of Stimson's feet came at Melody's legs, long heels dug into her shin, but she gripped tighter and her strong thigh muscles held the supports. Then Stimson made a mistake. She lunged at Melody's flapping hair, grabbed it and pulled Melody's head towards her.

Melody let go with both hands. Arching up with her burning core muscles, she took hold of Stimson's jacket and heaved backwards. She felt the jerk as Stimson's grip was pulled from the passenger handle inside the cockpit, and felt the stroke of soft fur slip past her face. Then she hung upside down by her legs and watched as Stimson plummeted to the earth below. Her arms and legs flailed as she grew smaller then hit the ground in a cloud of dust.

———

Frank and Reg met the plane when it had finished taxiing.

They stood beside the Audi side by side as equals, and welcomed their remaining team member back to the ground with open jaws and arms.

Melody stepped away from the wing quite dishevelled, but not shaken. She reached back into the aircraft and held out her hand. Angel jumped down. She'd been crying but was quiet. She wore the same pink pyjama bottoms with a red coat, and carried the same little pink backpack.

"That was insane, Melody," said Reg.

"That was above the call of duty, Mills," said Frank.

Melody breathed out long and slow, bent and picked up the little girl.

"The buddha?" asked Frank.

"Adeo," said Melody.

"The Porsche has gone," said Reg, looking at the line of cars outside the quiet airfield offices. "It was there when we came in, I'm sure of it."

Melody let her head fall back and closed her eyes.

"It wasn't for nothing. You did a brave thing, Melody," said Frank.

"It feels like it was for nothing, sir," she replied. She moved closer to Frank. "This little girl's mother just died." There was compassion in Melody's eyes.

Frank moved in closer to Melody. "This little girl's mother just caused the death of two of our team and countless others," he said, then pulled back and looked directly into her eyes. "You're a hero, and I'm damn proud to have you on my team, Mills."

"So would Harvey be," said Reg. "I don't think even he could have pulled that stunt."

"Thanks, boys," she whispered.

Angel clutched onto Melody's leg and buried her face in her cargo pants. Melody looked back at Frank, who raised his eyebrows, but didn't make any attempt to pull the girl way.

Melody smiled then gave a little laugh, which made Reg and Frank smile.

"I'm sorry to ask," said the pilot. "I was hired for the day, will I be needed?"

Frank's smile grew into a full laugh, hearty, from his chest. The pilot looked shocked at the reaction after what had just happened.

"Go, while you can," said Frank. "If we need you we can pull your name from the office, right?"

"Yeah, they know me, I fly here every week," said the pilot. "The name's Lord, Jason Lord."

24

THE BEAST REBORN

THE FALL TO THE WATER WAS JUST EIGHT METRES BUT IT felt like Harvey had landed on concrete. He released the zip on the explosive vest as soon as he hit the water, before he'd stopped spinning in the water's turbulence, before he'd thought about breathing and before he'd looked for Al Sayan.

Any second now.

He pulled the vest off and pushed it below him. He didn't stop to watch the current take it away. He just swam for his life.

He had to get away from it.

The explosion rocked his very core down to his internal organs. His bones felt as if they would snap. The sound of the river went quiet, and the searing pain through his head cast a black shadow over everything.

The fast flowing current rushed him away, washing him free of the place and the memories.

Harvey Stone surfaced two hundred metres down the river. The cold wind that rushed across the water woke him from death with a start, and he coughed up brown water. He felt as if his body was broken. He was unable to move his limbs and just lay on the surface taking in air.

Several minutes later, he'd travelled a mile down the river and began to shiver. Shock and the cold set in, which caused a severe reaction within his body. He shook. Not just his fingers or his hands, but his entire arms violently and uncontrollably fought to keep the circulation going. His lower lip trembled, and his lungs stung with each cold breath.

Was this the end? Had it happened already? The world glided past silently. Had it been that simple? After everything he'd done, it was over in seconds. Harvey knew he was alive. He also knew that all he had to do was close his eyes and all the pain, all the memories and all the lies would go away.

Nobody would remember him five years from now. He played a part in the game and his time was up. Could be up.

Do I have a choice?

Can I fight this?

Surely not, I can close my eyes and drift away.

I'm drifting already, it's easy. I don't have to try.

But what if there's more?

Harvey tried to stretch his arms out wide, but his joints ached and told him so by sending electric pulses along his nervous system.

My body is broken. How can I try?

He filled his lungs with air to keep him afloat.

My insides are damaged, I can't go on.

I can go on.

I don't want to go on.

You haven't tried.

But I have suffered.

You need to try. Take a step.

He began to flex his fingers.

You'll need more than fingers. One more step.

But I can close my eyes.

You're strong.

Not right now.

You've always been strong.

Let me sleep.

You can bend your arms.

Harvey slowly bent one arm beneath the water, then the other.

It's not over.

Have I made my choice?

I can do it.

There's no going back.

I've made my choice.

You're Harvey Stone.

I'm Harvey Stone.

Harvey found the movement in his limbs painful as thoughts of giving up washed over him and were taken out to sea. Though painful, his legs moved freely. He began to bend his arms back and forth. He moved his toes inside his wet boots and lay on his back to stretch his muscles. But he still shook. The water was viscously cold.

He'd come close to death, and he knew it. Harvey felt that when death held him in his hand, he was warmed. He couldn't remember the shivers, the biting cold or stinging skin. He had let death pass through him then banished him, and now suffered the penance.

Harvey watched the sky pass by above him, unsure if the sky was moving or if he was moving. Perhaps both. He wondered how far he'd travelled, but didn't recognise anything when he turned his head to see. There were no tall buildings, just factories and warehouses.

How far did I float?

That was when his head hit a rock.

The dull thump sent white light across his eyes, and he scrambled in the water. Blood trickled across his wet face, mingling with the water. He felt stones beneath him. *He heard footsteps on the stones.*

Harvey span and his vision caught up a second later, then a wave of blood ran through his bruised mind. Harvey focused on the stones beneath his hands. He brought a leg up and dug it into the gravel. He slowly raised his head.

Nobody was coming.

But a man was walking away.

Al Sayan.

He survived.

Harvey pushed his body upright, bringing his head slowly up. His legs were trembling and his fingers shook. He squeezed his hands tight then flexed his fingers.

He took a step.

He's getting away.

Another step.

Come on, Harvey Stone.

Harvey's wet boots sank into the gravelly beach. His bruised thigh pumped dull aches through his leg and his muscle tensed with every step. He pushed hard. He wasn't looking at Al Sayan who was moving fast now away from him. Harvey focused on the next step, then the next. He built a rhythm. Slowly, each step came with a short, sharp exhale of used air, spent. He sucked in more, took another step, let the pain run through him. Then more until the pain was pleasant. He welcomed the dull ache. He welcomed his body's rejection of movement. He forced his legs to move and his arms to pump, then he reached the grass. Soft, muddy grass.

Al Sayan was a distant shape two or three hundred metres away. Harvey didn't care, couldn't care. He had to keep moving away from the beach. Harvey could take long steps. They got faster. He looked ahead. Another man with Al Sayan. A small white van beside them both.

Heat.

The man went down. Harvey saw Al Sayan raise a rock high above his head. Harvey ran. The feeling was alien at first. A slow jog, but faster than the slow stumble.

Al Sayan brought the rock down on the man.

Harvey stepped faster. His legs trembled like he'd ran a marathon but his arms pumped.

Al Sayan opened the van door.

A dog barked and ran from nowhere, passing Harvey.

Harvey ran on. The dog leapt at Al Sayan and caught his leg as he was climbing into the driver's seat. Harvey heard a yelp, then the dog launched again.

Not far.

The dog snapped at Al Sayan and pinned him to the seat. Small, sharp bites on his legs and fingers. Harvey began to hear the frantic screams of Al Sayan from inside the car. His legs lashed out at the dog, who relaunched his attack.

Harvey stepped up to the fight and surprised the little dog. It took one look at Harvey and moved to sit beside his owner's body.

Al Sayan tried to straighten himself up and pull his legs into the van, but Harvey stood on his foot, took hold of the door and swung it hard against his leg, again and again. The Afghan bent double and reached for his leg. He didn't cry out. In Harvey's experience, men who know that death is coming rarely do. As Al Sayan reached forwards, Harvey grabbed hold of him and wrenched him from the vehicle onto the mud. The man tried to crawl away but found himself being dragged backwards.

Harvey hoisted him up into the van and slammed the doors.

The dog looked at Harvey with flattened ears, his head cocked to one side. His owner was dead. There was nothing Harvey could do. The dog was a collie. A white stripe ran the length of its nose between his eyes and ears, and finished on top of his head. The rest of his face was a mix of black and brown.

"What do you say there boy?" said Harvey lazily. "You staying or coming?" The dog looked at his owner. The back of the man's head had been caved in. "You getting in?"

"Good boy," said Harvey and opened the passenger door for the dog, who jumped in and sat down. The keys were in the ignition, and the engine was still warm. Within one minute, Harvey had warmth on his feet and legs and some semblance of human feeling returned to him.

Harvey found first gear and took the little diesel van along the bumpy track that led away from the river towards the road. Road signs told Harvey where he was and he made his way through the town of Rainham, then Hornchurch, then Romford. The sights became more familiar, the trees seemed greener, and the fields of Essex soon replaced the dirty buildings of London.

25

HEROES SONG

It was a typically overcast day at the East London cemetery. Melody and Reg stood either side of Frank, and together they stood among the friends and family of Denver Cox. His mother sat at the front dressed in a smart black dress, a black hat and veil, and black gloves.

There was no coffin, no dug earth. There was just a head-stone to remind the world of Denver's existence, and give his mother and his family a place to go and visit him, to talk to him, to remember him and grieve.

Melody would need no headstone to remember Denver. He had been a solid man, true and reliable. She stood and listened to the vicar reading from the Bible, and remembered how Denver had talked her down from bursting into the barn when Donny Cartwright had been running a human traf-ficking ring. Denver had always been quiet until push came to the shove, and then he always stepped up.

Denver's family took turns to talk of him, and Melody delighted in hearing about her friend, things he'd done as a child, antics, his passion for speed and adrenaline. Even at a young age Denver went go-cart racing and displayed an almost fearless trust in his own capabilities. His mother explained how she had watched him take corners at high speeds and had to look away.

Nobody spoke of Denver's love for supercars, and how that passion had come very close to putting him behind bars. There was no need to mention it. He hadn't gone to prison and had formed a career from doing the things he loved the most.

The vicar asked the assembly if anybody else would like to say a few words.

Frank stepped forward.

He addressed the gathering of friends and family but spoke directly to Denver's mother.

"I've met many men in my time in this world in many countries, cities, and towns. Some come and go, while others stay a while. Denver was an honest man, true to his word and one of the most reliable," said Frank. Denver's mother nodded. "I firmly believe that the people we meet, new faces that enter our lives and share our time, fall into three categories. Some we meet for a reason; some twist of fate guides the purpose of the meeting for the benefit of them or me, and then they move on, or I move on. Fate is fulfilled. Denver does not fall into this category." Frank took a breath and paused to let the words sink into the engaged crowd.

"Others, we meet for a season; a brief period of time, summer, winter or a year or two, where two people become friends, enemies, colleagues, and then fate again sends one or both of us along a different path. Denver does not belong in this category." Frank cleared his throat and stood strong, though Melody could see that he was holding his emotions together.

"There's some people we meet that do not cross our paths for a reason or a season, they join us for a lifetime. These people are few and far between." Frank took his eyes away from Mrs Cox and looked at Melody and Reg. "But these people are exceptional, and some subconscious inside us, in our very cores, knows that we will love these people forever, and no matter what happens, we will be by their sides when times are good, and we will offer our shoulders when times are difficult. Regardless of the circumstance, and regardless of the outcomes, we will be together, and that person will be a part of our lives forever. Denver Cox is one of those people. I'm proud to say he will always be a part of my life, for as long I still breathe."

Mrs Cox wiped tears away as Frank stepped down from the small astroturf podium, and rejoined Melody and Reg. He put his arm around Melody's shoulder. Melody wiped her eyes with a small handkerchief.

The congregation were invited to join Denver's family at their home for his wake. As soon as the people began to move, Denver's father stood and approached the team. He stopped directly in front of them all and shook their hands one by one, looking each of them in the eye.

"Denver died doing what he loved the most," said Mr Cox.

"He's a hero, sir," said Reg. "I'll never forget what he did."

"You were there?"

"I was, sir."

Mr Cox nodded and put his hand on Reg's shoulder. He turned to Frank.

"Thank you for the kind words, Mr Carver."

"It was nothing that isn't true, Mr Cox."

"So you're the team he spoke about then, are you?" said Mr Cox, in an attempt to cheer the conversation. "I thought there were more of you?"

"We were five," began Frank. "But we lost-"

"We lost the best driver and pilot I ever met," said a voice from behind them. "He was a hell of a man."

Melody spun around at the sound of the voice.

"I'm sorry, who are you?" said Mr Cox.

"Stone, sir. Harvey Stone." Harvey held out his hand for Mr Cox. "I'm very sorry your loss. Denver was one of my closest friends."

26

ALIVE

THE TEAM SAT IN THE MEETING ROOM OF HEADQUARTERS. Reg sat on one of the two couches, Melody stood by the coffee machine, and Harvey leaned against the door. There was a hole in the room where Denver used to sit on the arm of the other couch.

The dog had visited the team individually and received pats on the head. He'd got a lot of cuddles and attention from Melody, then went to sit at Harvey's feet.

Angel sat beside Melody on a little chair. She was colouring in a pad with an array of pens and pencils, oblivious to the people around her. Melody had bought the young girl a new dress and had cleaned her from her ordeal as a prisoner.

Frank addressed the team.

"Today's debrief will be slightly different, aside from the addition of our two guests," said Frank. He shifted his feet, looked up and stared at the team, one by one.

"I'm taking Angel to the child services today, sir," said Melody. "They've found a home for her."

"Good, she'll need a lot of care after what she's been through."

"She's a strong kid, sir."

Frank turned to Harvey.

Harvey didn't reply.

"And have you found the mutt a home, Stone?"

"Yeah, as it happens, I have."

"Good, I'm glad," said Frank, then turned back to the room. "Today's discussion will not involve us mourning Denver, though we all do mourn him inside. The day will not even involve us celebrating his glorious death, though we are all grateful for his heroic actions." Reg leaned forward in the seat, and Melody stared at Frank, hanging on his words.

"We will, of course, assess our successes, our failures and compile our reports. It's part of the job, but I'd also like to hear from you all. I'd like to know where your hearts are, and where we stand as a team." The last sentence was spoken softly.

There was silence.

"Let's start with a recap of suspects." Frank picked up a whiteboard marker and turned to the board.

"Stimson," he whispered to avoid letting Angel hear her mother's name.

"Nailed," said Reg. "Courtesy of Melody Mills." Harvey looked across at her and nodded his approval. Frank wrote beside Stimson's name *Deceased*.

"Larson, status?"

"Nailed," said Reg. "Courtesy of our very own, back from the dead, Harvey Stone." Reg hammered out a drumbeat on his knees.

"Hague?" asked Frank, ignoring Reg's enthusiasm.

"Deceased, sir," said Melody.

"Not doing too well so far, are we?"

"Adeo, Stimson's minder," called Frank. "Did we find him?"

Melody and Reg were silent.

Frank turned back to face the room. "And I assume we believe the priceless jade buddha is with him?"

"That's correct, sir."

"So the case remains open." Frank stared at Melody. "Until further notice." He turned to Harvey. "I want the man found."

"Yes, sir," said Melody.

"You should know," began Frank again, "that your actions, though unrecognised with respect to Al Sayan, have not gone unnoticed where it counts."

"Sir?" asked Reg.

"We found the missing two taxi drivers in a locked room inside the Stratford warehouse. They were alive, and we've been credited with their release. My superiors sent an email thanking us for our efforts throughout the entire operation, and also sent condolences for the loss of Denver."

"Sounds cold, sir," said Melody. "Would have been nice to hear it from the horse's mouth."

Frank didn't reply to Melody. Instead, he carried on with his talk.

"Okay, like I said, we're going to discuss how we're feeling, where are we as a team. It's been a long few days and we've all been through more than our fair share of trauma."

Angel began to tug on Melody's sleeve.

"Not now, sweetheart," said Melody.

"Sir," began Reg, "what about Al Sayan? And the taxi driver, and the tech guy?"

"That's not our case, Tenant," replied Frank. "We can't take credit for a case that doesn't fall under our jurisdiction. He was collateral." Frank held his gaze until Reg turned away.

"But, sir–"

"No buts, I'm afraid. SO10 and SO19 took the credit for the takedown of all three terrorist suspects. Please omit them from your reports. You will, however, be asked to provide a statement surrounding Denver's actions at a later date."

The team fell quiet.

"So, how are we feeling?" asked Frank.

Nobody replied.

"Melody, you usually have something to say, where's your heart at?"

Melody didn't reply.

"Team, I'm not asking you open up here, I'm looking to gauge the motivation. And right now, quite understandably, it's on the floor." He paused. "Am I right?"

"It's pretty hard to think about the future, sir," said Reg.

Frank pointed at him. "Good, keep it coming."

Melody looked confused. "You seriously want to hear how mad we are that we lost a friend and failed to solve the case?"

"Yes, tell me." Frank was loud, excited and enthusiastic at hearing their dejected tones.

"Okay, well, we're upset we lost Denver," said Melody.

"Understandable," said Frank. "So am I. Next."

"We're mad that we didn't recover the buddha," said Reg.

"Good, *why* are you mad?"

Reg looked at Melody for support.

"It's the first case we lost, sir."

"*Yes*," cried Frank. "Yes it was. So what are you going to *do* about it?"

The team were stunned by Frank's outburst, it had been a sombre few days.

"You're going to go find it, right?"

Melody caught on to Franks encouragement. "Yes, sir," she shouted.

"*Good*," said Frank. "And what happens when we can't find it?" Franks voice rose in volume.

"We look harder, sir."

"Excellent, Tenant. Are we going to fail?"

"No, sir," both Melody and Reg called out.

"Fantastic. Denver doesn't want you sitting in here moping. Get out there and make it happen." Frank pointed to the door.

Angel began to pull on Melody's sleeve again.

"Angel, let me talk please."

"But look," said Angel.

Melody glanced down at the girl, who had pulled some colouring pencils from her little pink backpack. "Not now, darling,"

"This isn't mine," said Angel, and shrugged. "Where did it come from?" Angel said the words slowly, as young girls do.

Frank had turned away and was summarising the status of the deceased suspects on the whiteboard. Reg was fiddling with an iPad, but Harvey was looking directly at Angel.

He smiled when he caught a glimpse of green.

Melody caught his smile and followed his gaze.

Angel stood by her side with a two-thousand-year-old jade buddha in her hands.

27

A GIFT FROM THE BEAST

FRANK DROVE, AND HARVEY SAT IN THE PASSENGER SEAT. Harvey was dressed in clean cargo pants, new boots and a clean white t-shirt beneath his old leather jacket. They drove out of town and headed into the green suburbs of Essex. The dog was in the back seat.

"Are we heading anywhere in particular, Stone?"

"I thought we might take a stroll, Frank."

"Could have done that by the river, couldn't we?"

"I want to show you something," said Harvey.

"Sounds nice. Are you going to tell me what happened?"

"What happened?"

"We thought you were dead, Stone. We saw the explosion. Nobody could have survived that."

"It was close, maybe the closest I've ever been."

"It's almost a miracle, Stone, not just close."

"Depends on your point of view," replied Harvey. "I haven't given it much thought since. How are you feeling?"

"Feeling?"

"You asked the team how we're feeling, nobody asked

you," replied Harvey. "How are you feeling? Are you motivated?"

"Motivated enough to fight another day. Are you offering encouragement?"

"In a way," said Harvey. "Turn here."

Frank steered the car toward Theydon Bois.

"Do you have closure, Frank?"

"Closure?"

"Yes, closure. Do you feel like Jan can rest in peace? Do you feel like you avenged her death?"

"In a way, it hasn't sunk in yet. What with-"

"Denver, right," finished Harvey. "Do you feel like the noose has lifted, or relaxed a little?"

"My noose?"

"Yes, Frank, your noose. We both wore them. Yours woke you up at night, didn't it? It dragged you to work every day, and it reminded you daily that someone out there somewhere was responsible for your wife's death. It reminded you that you lived and breathed another day on the planet in the same country, city even, and that you shared the same air as him." Harvey paused. "The noose was tight, wasn't it?"

"It was, Stone, yes."

"Forget the formalities, Frank, I'm Harvey. I think we know each other well enough now," said Harvey. "Tell me how you feel, how tight the noose is. Maybe I can help." Harvey looked across at the older man. "I'm an expert at dealing with nooses, Frank. Remember?"

"You want the truth?" Frank asked.

"Of course."

"I can't remember when I last slept a solid night."

"Thought so."

"You can tell?"

"I told you, I'm an expert."

"I don't think I'll *ever* get closure. I don't think I'll ever understand how one human being can be responsible for the deaths of so many others."

"It's a cruel world, Frank."

"Yes, yes it is, Harvey," replied Frank. "How about you? You were typically quiet in the meeting."

"Planning," said Harvey.

"Planning?" asked Frank.

"And patience. The two go hand in hand in my experience. Turn right here."

Frank indicated and turned.

"You going to tell me what it was you were planning?" asked Frank.

"My future."

"Your future?"

Harvey didn't reply.

"Your future is with the unit, Harvey. We need you now more than ever."

"Perhaps," said Harvey. "Perhaps not. Whatever I decide, it needs to be my decision."

"Your decision? It's always-"

"I need you take my noose off me, Frank."

"Okay."

"You want commitment? Release me, give me a choice. You want to see what I'm capable of, set me free. Some birds are just not meant to be caged, Frank."

"I take it you got the answers you were looking for?"

"I got answers, not necessarily the ones I wanted to hear, but I can put the rest together myself."

"Did you ever suspect Julios?"

"Never, he was my one ally."

"I'm sorry."

"Don't be," Said Harvey. "He's dead, they're dead. I'm alive, you're alive."

"So how does your future look?"

"Fresh start, deeper sleep," said Harvey.

"Deeper sleep?"

"Peace, Frank." Harvey paused. "I'm not sure I ever knew what it was."

"So if it was Julios after all this time, who killed Julios? Are you any closer to finding that out?" Frank glanced across at Harvey's face, but it was typically impassive.

"I'll find him. He's on my list. But I'll take my time."

"I'm pleased for you, Harvey," began Frank, before pushing the conversation forward, "I'm pleased you finally found the answers, even if the truth wasn't ideal."

"Ideal, Frank?"

"You know what I mean," said Frank, "you got your closure. You worked hard at it, and there's plenty of people who never thought you would."

"I have you to thank, Frank," said Harvey.

"I didn't solve anything."

"You held the noose tight, that's what I'm saying. I don't need the noose anymore. It's detrimental to my future now."

"It's detrimental?" asked Frank. "But if I set you free, if I tear up the arrest warrant, would that be detrimental to the team?"

"You want the truth from me?"

"Of course."

"I feel part of something, Frank. When Denver died, I feel like we all lost something. I've seen men lost to crime. They've bled out or had their heads blown off, but I never felt loss. Not like-"

"Like Denver?"

"Yeah, not like Denver."

"Turn here, Frank."

"But this is-"

"John Cartwright's house, yes."

"What are we doing here?"

"Taking a walk, showing you something." Harvey sighed. "Letting you in, I guess."

"Letting me in?"

"You wanted to see where my noose was tied."

"I thought I held the rope?" asked Frank.

"You tightened the knot. The rope has always been tied to this place."

Frank stopped the car beside the little groundsman's house. It was where Harvey had lived when he worked for his foster father, John Cartwright.

"Needs some care and attention, doesn't it?" said Frank, looking at the broken windows, overgrown ivy and graffiti on the front door.

"Don't we all." Harvey climbed out the car, let the dog out, and started walking along the little stream that ran through the grounds of the three-hundred-acre property. Frank followed and caught up with the younger man. The dog ran ahead, drank from the stream and bounded in the long wild grass.

"Are you keeping him?" asked Frank, referring to the dog.

"Was thinking about it, or maybe gift him to Melody. They both need some love and attention."

"What you going to call him?"

"Boon."

"Boon?" asked Frank. "Why Boon?"

"It's a name, and I found him the boonies, in the middle of nowhere." Harvey paused. "This is where Hannah and I played as children," he said without looking at the older man.

"Lucky kids," said Frank.

"We made the best of a bad situation. Our parents were murdered, remember?"

Frank didn't reply.

"We used to climb that willow there and pretend to be pirates. Our names are carved in the bark somewhere."

"Fond memories?"

"The only memories I've got, Frank," said Harvey. "At least, the only ones I wish to remember."

"You're different now. You've changed, Harvey."

"Things happen, people adapt."

"No, not adapting. You really have found peace, haven't you?"

"I think so, Frank. That's why I need the noose removed."

"Okay. That's easy, Harvey."

"It's gone?"

"It's gone."

"No more threat of prison?"

"I'll tear the warrant up as soon as we're back."

Harvey didn't reply.

"Feel good?"

Harvey nodded. "Want me to remove yours?"

"My what?"

"Your noose."

"Mine's tight."

"That's what I thought, *I* can ease the knot, *you* can take it off yourself."

"How are you going to do that?"

"You remember the basement here?"

"How can I forget? Its history is full of-"

"Closure, Frank," said Harvey. "Its history is steeped in closure."

Frank didn't reply.

"Why don't you go take a look down there?" asked Harvey. "I'll wait here."

"And what will I find?"

"You remember once, we discussed the obligations of society, and how sometimes a man's crime is so severe that society is obligated to punish him?"

"I remember," said Frank. His heart began to beat harder as the tone of Harvey's voice fell into a cruel, cold tone.

"And do you remember how we discussed that, some-times, it is those that have suffered the most who are obliged to enact that punishment?"

Frank was quiet, his breath held. "Al Sayan?" he whispered.

Harvey didn't reply.

The End.

END OF BOOK STUFF

Stone Rage - Book Four - Chapter One.

"What the hell are we doing out here, Les?"

"This is where the boss said to meet them,"

"Its pitch black mate, I can't see anything, there could be fifty of them out there."

"Stop being paranoid," said Les, "it's not like you to be a bit jumpy."

"I'm not jumpy, I just don't trust them dirty, sly little-"

"We'll be out of here before you know it," replied Les, "chill out. I used to bring the birds over here-"

"Over here? What for? The place gives me the creeps, can we at least have the heater on, it's freezing?"

"Why do *think* I brought them here?" said Les turning the Jaguar's temperature dial up, "A bit of rough and tumble, Jay, they loved it."

"Is that what they told you? How many of them came back for a second night of creepy love in the freaky field?"

"Not many," Laughed Les, "well, one actually, a few times. Sticky Sarah we used to call her, she used to like that people could see in, dirty cow, voyeurism I think they call that."

"Sticky Sarah?"

"Yeah, strange girl she was, had a great set, but she *was* a bit weird."

"Les, nothing about what you just said is normal. Firstly why was she called Sticky Sarah?"

"Well, it was more like a tacky really, but the name Tacky Sarah didn't work-"

"Oh right, and when you say, 'We,' can I assume that you weren't the only one to experience Sticky Sarah's tacky sensation?"

"No, we all had a go, well, most of us, apart from Little Lee, poor fella was a slow developer, I have no idea how that guy survived childhood, he's probably still a virgin now."

"And when you say that Sticky Sarah used to enjoy being watched, do you mean to say that you brought her over here and banged her in the back of your car so other blokes could see in?"

"Yeah, dog walkers and stuff, she loved it." Said Les.

"Did that not ever strike you as a bit weird, Les?"

"Not really,"

Jay looked away from him in disgust, "I can't see shit out there," he muttered, "what was it anyway?"

"What was what?"

"The car, what car did you have?"

"Well, you know, I was young, didn't have enough money for my own car."

"Don't tell me you used your mum's car to smash Sticky Sarah around and have a load of dirty of pervs stand around-"

"No, no, no, I never," Said Les, " I have got *some* decency,"

"So who's car was it?"

"I don't bloody know do I,"

"You nicked it?"

"Yeah, of course I did, had a different one each week. I learned to drive in a nicked motor, my old man taught me."

"You what?" said Jay, "Your old man taught you to drive in a stolen car?"

"Yeah, he didn't *know* it was stolen, I told him I'd borrowed it off a mate,"

"What if he got caught? How would you explain that?"

"Behave, Jay, I was fifteen years old, I didn't know any better."

"You're something else, you know that?"

Les laughed, "It's been a good old life, Jay. Had some great times I have."

"Don't get all teary on me now,"

"No, you know what I mean, don't you ever wonder?"

"Wonder what?"

"You know, if you died, have you done all the things you wanted to do?"

"I done most of them, Les," Said Jay, there's a few things still on the list though, one day I'll get around to ticking them off."

"Whats that then?"

"Well, I might see if Sticky Sarah is still around and see if she fancies a bunk up while some old perv knocks one out,"

Both side windows exploded sending glass all over the two men. Big hands reached in and dragged the two men through the car windows. Les pulled a knife and slashed blindly at the two huge men who pinned him down on the grass. One of the men, a bald man with tattoos on his face, held Les' throat tightly and the other stopped his knife hand waving around by standing on his arm. A large knee came down onto Les' chest and one by one, each of the fingers that held the knife were wrenched up, bent backwards and broken.

Les screamed in pain, he struggled, but it was useless against the size and weight of the man on top of him. Eventually the last finger was snapped back like a twig and the knife was taken from him.

The smaller of the two bald men that pinned him down held the knife curiously. He turned it in his hands, put the point in Les' eye, and slowly pushed down until the blade entered Les' brain and he fell silent.

Jay was the other side of the car. Strong arms held him against the Jaguars sleek paintwork. No words were spoken. Jay stopped struggling.

A tall, willowy man in a long overcoat stepped from the darkness into the pale moonlight. Jay could barely make out the features of his face, but saw the glint of a scar that ran from the man's eye to his mouth, through his lips and down his chin to his throat.

The man gave a gesture to the men that stood beside Les' body to open the car boot. The two men opened the boot and removed the sports holdall that contained the four kilos of cocaine. They checked it and returned the nod to the boss.

Jay stared up at the man and spat.

"You will take a message to your boss."

"Fuck you, send a letter."

One of the men holding Jay landed a huge fist on Jay's nose. Jay felt the bone break and tasted blood almost immediately.

"I am a reasonable man, but I *am* a businessman. It seems like your boss and I are in the same business. Competition."

"So run a sale or something, isn't that what business men do?"

"It's an option," The man replied, "But I prefer not to cut profits for the sake of a few easy sales. I prefer to cut the competition." The man reached inside his coat and pulled out a long fillet knife. He flexed the blade and ran his finger along the thin steel.

"You will deliver the message for me?" asked the man.

"I'll tell him some ugly bloke from some shit stink part of

Europe wants his balls cut off," said Jay, "how does that sound, wanker?"

"Hold him," the man said calmly.

The two men either side of Jay grabbed his hair and held him tight. The man in the coat stepped forward and ran the side of the blade across Jay's nose. Then with one hand, he pulled Jay's ear out from his head, and with the other, sliced through the tissue and gristle in two neat, clean slices. Jay screamed and struggled against the two much larger men, but couldn't move. Spit flew from gritted teeth and his eyes were clamped shut as he fought the searing pain. He felt the man pull on his other ear, dull and hard. He felt the blade touch his skin, sharp. Then he felt nothing but the burn of where his ears once were.

"Make sure he doesn't lose those, he may need them one day." Said the man in the coat as wiped the blood from the blade onto Jay's jacket.

Jay's knees had given way, his weight was easily supported by the two men. They dropped him to the floor face first, then kicked him to roll him over. Jay pulled his hands to head, but his wounds was too tender to touch, blood had ran across his face into his eyes. He felt his arms being tugged outward. Then felt a sharp point in the palm of his hand. He glared helplessly through the sticky blood to see one of the large men with a cordless drill. Then he felt the screw tear through his tendons, fixing one of his ears to his open hand with a long, gold coloured screw.

GET J.D.WESTON'S STARTER LIBRARY FOR FREE

Stay up to date with the Stone Cold Thriller series and get FREE eBooks sent straight to your inbox.

Visit www.jdweston.com for details.

ALSO BY J.D. WESTON.

The Stone Cold Thriller Series.

Novellas

The Alaskan Adventure

.

APPRECIATION

If you enjoyed Stone Cold, please do help me to continue Harvey's story by leaving an honest review.

A few short lines about your experience with the book can be all it takes to help a future reader discover the series.

Many thanks.

J.D. Weston

To learn more about J.D. Weston

www.jdweston.com
john@jdweston.com

A NOTE FROM THE AUTHOR

The Stone Cold Thriller series is set in East London and Essex and features places from my own childhood.

While many of the buildings, pubs and streets are fictitious, some of the more prominent locations in the series are borne from my own life experience and are as accurate as my memory allows.

My family are from Theydon Bois, where John Cartwright's house is located. In fact, my parents lived in the great house before I was born, renting a room off the wealthy owner.

The headquarters building is based on the same road as my first flat in Silvertown.

In the first book, Stone Cold, the location of the first murder was in fact in the same building as my first job.

While the locations may offer an insight into my own childhood, and early working years, the characters are all fictitious. I recently handed the first draft of book one, Stone Cold to some family members and discovered that John Cartwright is, in fact, the name of my great-grandfather. I hope that he wasn't into the things the character John Cartwright is, and if he was, I'd like to know where the money went.

Stone Cold sets the scene for the rest of the series and is the result of a considerable amount of research. I tried to understand what books were out there, what people wanted and, of course, what I wanted to write.

I do hope you've enjoyed the series so far, but more than that, I hope you've grown to feel for Harvey and the other characters, and if you've come this far, perhaps you'll come a little further and see how the next part of Harvey's story unfolds. I wish I could tell you, I'm itching to just blurt it out. But hey, where's the fun in that?

To learn more about J.D. Weston

www.jdweston.com
john@jdweston.com

STONE COLD

Book One of the Stone Cold Thriller series

One priceless set of diamonds. Three of London's ruthless east end crime families. One very angry assassin with a hit list.

Harvey Stone has questions that someone will answer. Who killed his parents and why? Who raped and killed his sister? And why are his closest allies hiding the truth.

When Harvey is asked to kill east London's biggest crime boss in return for one name on his list, there is only one answer.

Can Harvey survive the gang war, untangle the web of deceit and uncover the truth behind his sisters death?

Stone Cold is the first book in the Stone Cold thriller series. If you enjoy fast-paced adventure, gritty vigilante stories and no-nonsense heroes, then you'll love J.D. Weston's brand new Thriller Series.

Unlock the Stone Cold Thriller Series with the first book, Stone Cold.

STONE FURY

Book Two of the Stone Cold Thriller series

The lives of twelve young girls are being sold. The seller is on Harvey Stone's hit list.

When ex-hitman Harvey Stone learns of a human trafficking ring taking place in his old stomping ground, he is sickened. But when he learns the name of the person running the show, an opportunity arises to cross one more name of his list.

Can Harvey save the ill-fated girls, and serve justice to those who are most deserved?

Stone Fury is the second book in the Stone Cold thriller series.

If you enjoy fast-paced adventure, gritty vigilante stories and no-nonsense heroes, then you'll love J.D. Weston's brand new Thriller Series.

Click here now to get early access to the next part of Harvey's puzzle.

STONE FALL

Book Three of the Stone Cold Thriller series

One evil terrorist with a plan to change the face of London. A missing child, and one priceless jade Buddha. Only Harvey Stone and his team of organised crime specialists can prevent disaster.

When Harvey and the team intercept a heist to rob a priceless jade Buddha, little did they know they would be uncovering a terrorist attack on London's St Paul's Cathedral, and a shocking hostage scenario.

Can Harvey and the team stop the terrorists, save the little girl and rescue the priceless Buddha?

Stone Fall is the third book in the Stone Cold thriller series. If you enjoy fast-paced adventure, gritty vigilante stories and no-nonsense heroes, then you'll love J.D. Weston's brand new Thriller Series.

Buy now to read the next adventure in the Stone Cold thriller series.

STONE RAGE

Book Four of the Stone Cold Thriller series

Two of east London's most notorious gangs go head to head with the Albanian mafia, and one angry assassin who's out to clean up.

When Harvey Stone is sent undercover to put a stop a turf war between the Albanian mafia and two of East London's most notorious gangs, nobody expected him to be welcomed like a hero by an old face.

Has Harvey finally gone rogue, or will he put a stop to the bloodshed once and for all?

Stone Rage is the fourth book in the Stone Cold thriller series.

If you enjoy fast-paced adventure, gritty vigilante stories and no-nonsense heroes, then you'll love J.D. Weston's brand new Thriller Series.

Buy now and get your hands on Harvey's next adventure in the Stone Cold thriller series.

STONE FREE

Book Five of the Stone Cold Thriller series

Death by internet. A mind blowing masterplan, where death holds all the cards.

Harvey Stone plays guardian angel on international soil when two governments prepare to do battle, and the lives of innocent people are at stake.

Can Harvey free the condemned women and avert an international disaster. Can he defy all odds and escape alive? Find out in Stone Free, the fifth book in the Stone Cold Thriller series.

If you enjoy intense thrillers, with shocking storylines, then you'll love this new series from J.D. Weston.

Get stuck into the Stone Cold Thriller series, get Stone Free now.

97638035R10154

Made in the USA
Middletown, DE
06 November 2018